The Experiment

Journeys to
FAYRAH

---

1. *The Portal*
2. *The Experiment*

The Experiment

Bill Myers

A. R.

Pts. _4.0_

RL _4.5_

IL _MG_

BETHANY HOUSE PUBLISHERS
MINNEAPOLIS, MINNESOTA 55438

Cover and inside illustrations by Andrea Jorgenson

Published by Bethany House Publishers
A Ministry of Bethany Fellowship, Inc.
6820 Auto Club Road, Minneapolis, Minnesota 55438

Printed in the United States of America

Library of Congress Cataloging-in-Publication Data

    Myers, Bill, 1953–
    The experiment / Bill Myers.
        p.   cm. — (Journeys to Fayrah ; bk. 2)
    Summary: Cross-dimensionalized to the land of Fayrah, where
they are confronted with realities that science cannot explain, Joshua
and Denise discover the meaning of God and his love.

    [1. Fantasy. 2. Christian life—Fiction.] I. Title.
II. Series: Myers, Bill, 1953–   Journeys to Fayrah ; bk. 2.
PZ7.M9823Ex   1991
[Fic]—dc20   91–19170
ISBN 1–55661–214–1   CIP
                                                                  AC

For Mackenzie . . .
Our newest joy
and my officemate
throughout this journey.

BILL MYERS is a superbly creative writer and film director who co-created the "McGee & Me" book and video series and whose work has received over two dozen national awards. His new *Journeys to Fayrah* is a remarkable series of exciting fantasy/mythical stories that totally captivate young readers (ages 8 and up). With an originality all his own, Myers builds in conflicts of good and evil, profound allegories that young people can grasp and apply to their own lives, and a timeless story that adults will love as well.

Contents

1. Another Day, Another Full Moon 9
2. Just Like Old Times . . . Sorta 17
3. Arrivals 29
4. The Weaver 39
5. A Guided Tour 51
6. The Machine 59
7. The Experiment Begins 71
8. Choices 83
9. The Sign 91
10. Another Last Chance 99
11. Fight of Love 109
12. Reunion 117
13. To the Rescue 129

— CHAPTER ONE —

ANOTHER DAY, ANOTHER FULL MOON

"I have not forgotten!" the harsh voice cawed. "You belong to me. I have not forgotten." For the hundredth time Denise looked up through the gnarled, twisted branches of the frozen forest, and for the hundredth time she saw the black leather-winged creature circling high overhead. Half woman, half who-knows-what, the animal was enough to give anybody the willies . . . even if that anybody knew they were only dreaming.

It had been exactly two months since Denise traveled to Fayrah and had first seen the creature. And for two months the ugly thing kept returning to her, haunting her in her dreams. But what made it even more frightening was that she had been hearing part of that voice, seeing some of that face for years . . . in earlier dreams . . . in earlier nightmares.

"Surely you've not forgotten?" the voice demanded.

Denise swallowed hard. It took her a moment to gather her courage, but she was finally able to shout, "What do you want from me? Leave me alone!"

Suddenly, the entire forest broke into mocking laughter. And more suddenly still Denise realized she wasn't standing in a forest, but sitting in her classroom.

"All I want from you, young lady, is to diagram this sentence." It was Mrs. Barnick, her English teacher. She stood three desks ahead of Denise with a less-than-pleased look on her face.

"Ahhh . . ." Denise stalled, desperately trying to push the dream out of her mind while she searched for the sentence. *What sentence? Where is it? On the blackboard? In the textbook?* There were giggles and whispers from all those around her. She could feel the tops of her ears start to burn like they always did when she got embarrassed.

"Denny," Mrs. Barnick spoke evenly as she pointed to the side board. "It's sentence number three, from yesterday's assignment . . . *The clown's humor was quite bizarre.*

Denise peered at the board.

"What is the subject of the sentence?" Mrs. Barnick persisted. "What is *bizarre*?"

"*She* is," a red-haired boy cracked from two rows over. Again the room broke into laughter. The boy grinned proudly at his sharp wit—that is, until his eyes met Denise's. Suddenly he realized what every other guy in Lincoln Elementary already knew. You didn't give Denise a rough time. Suddenly he realized that the sharp wit of his would probably earn him a bloody nose or a black eye—or maybe both. Unless an escape route could be found, the red-haired boy would soon experience the awful pain of hassling Denise Wolff.

Don't get me wrong. Since her return from Fayrah, Denise had come a long way toward controlling her temper. But self-control isn't learned overnight—a fact that would be all too evident to the clever red-haired boy.

"In the future, Denny," Mrs. Barnick said, "I suggest you do your sleeping at home."

"Yes, ma'am," Denise mumbled as the bell rang to end the class.

She gathered her books and crowded toward the door with the rest of the students. Of course there were the usual "way to go's" and "nice work, Denny's" from the kids who liked taking chances with their lives. But Denise didn't pay much attention. She figured the whole thing really wasn't her fault. She wasn't the one who'd put English at the end of the day. Who in their right mind would schedule the world's most boring subject for sixth period? No, make that the second most boring subject. She'd almost forgotten about math. Then of course there was geography, Spanish, science, and health.

But she scores so high on the tests, the counselors had told her mother.

If she'd just apply herself, she'd be an A-student, the teachers insisted.

"Yeah? Well let them try being a kid for a day," Denise grumbled as she shuffled down the hall toward her locker. "That'd show 'em. That'd show them all."

Instinctively she glanced around the hall for the red-haired boy. But he was no fool. Already he was headed for the exit door. Already he knew that it would be best to stay out of Denny's way—at least for the next couple of decades.

Denise threw her locker open, and started loading up with the evening's torture of homework when the thought suddenly struck her. *Wait a minute! Tonight's the night! Tonight we use the Bloodstone to signal the Fay-rahnians. Tonight I'll finally prove to Joshua that it wasn't just make-believe, or mass hysteria, or, how did he put it? ... "A couple of kids' overactive imaginations."*

With a dramatic flair she dumped the books back into her locker, slammed it shut, and headed for the next building—the middle school's gymnasium. The older kids would be there setting up their science projects. And since it involved science, that of course is where Josh would be.

"Hey, Denny!" It was Nathan, Josh's little brother. She slowed down to let him catch up. His limp was as painful to watch as ever. They'd both hoped it would disappear after their trip to Fayrah, after Denise had seen him without it in the Stream's reflection. But no such luck. It was still there, just as obvious as ever. Still, there were other changes. As with Denny, there were deeper changes . . .

For starters, Nathan was no longer the most selfish human being on the face of the planet. Oh, he still had his moments. Like Denise, there were still plenty of areas that needed work. But instead of a modern-day Scrooge, he was coming off more like your average run-of-the-mill savings and loan president. Not a great improvement, but a start.

"Listen, I might be late tonight."

"What?" Denny came to a stop. "Tonight's the full moon. If we don't signal them tonight—" She spotted a nearby group straining to eavesdrop, and lowered her voice. "If we don't signal them tonight we'll have to wait a whole 'nother month before—"

"I know, I know," Nathan interrupted. "But we're having a geography test tomorrow."

"So?"

"So Jerry Boleslavski's having a lousy time memorizing his state capitols."

"So?"

"So I'd promised to help."

"Nathan . . ."

"How'd I know our teacher was going to spring the test on us tomorrow?"

Denise took a deep breath. She refused to get angry. Worse things than this had happened, she was sure of it . . . although at the moment, she couldn't exactly put her finger on one.

"Look," Nathan insisted, "we'll get done in time, no sweat. But if I'm not there, you and Josh go ahead without me."

"You're kidding."

"No, I'm serious. There'll be other full moons."

"Nathan . . ."

Without a word, he turned his back on her and started hobbling down the hall.

"Nathan . . . Nathaniel . . ."

There was no answer.

Denny let out a sigh. The trip to Fayrah had improved some things about Nathan, but it sure hadn't done much for his stubbornness.

———

"Listen, kiddo," Josh said as kindly as possible. "I don't want you to be too disappointed when nothing happens."

"Oh, I won't," Denise said as they rounded the corner and headed up the street toward Grandpa O'Brien's Secondhand Shop. She couldn't help grinning as she fingered the Bloodstone inside her coat pocket. The full moon was already high overhead. In just a few minutes she'd expose the stone to its light, then she'd see what ol' Joshy boy had to say about "disappointments."

For the past couple of hours Josh had been dragging her around to see all the science projects, explaining what they were about and how they worked and everything. Josh loved science, and for him the hours flew. Denny hated science, and for her the hours crawled. But it wasn't a complete waste: during that time she had mastered the fine art of faking interest. In fact, she'd become quite an expert at using phrases like "No kidding," "I see," "That's neat," "Uh-huh," and "Wow!"

Denise didn't mind. Faking interest was a small price to pay for Josh's friendship—a friendship that had lasted almost as long as she could remember. It lasted through those awful months after her dad left home . . . it lasted through her slowly but surely becoming the school oddball . . . it even lasted through Josh having to constantly drag her away from the wisecracking bullies whose faces she kept pulverizing.

Yessir, if anybody qualified as a best friend, it was Joshua O'Brien. The only problem was he qualified as everybody's best friend. Smart, athletic, funny—everything came easy for him, maybe too easy—even making friends. That was why Denny admired him so much, and also why, on occasion, she couldn't stand him.

"Look, I'm not saying something didn't happen to you and Nathan," he continued, "something emotional, or even some sort of *natural phenomenon*. But all this talk about a Kingdom and an *Imager* and stuff—well, no offense, but it all sounds just a little too far out for me."

"And you don't believe in anything too far out."

"I believe in science—in cause and effect. But if you're expecting me to buy some sort of magic performed by some sort of . . ." he searched for the word, "some sort of Wizard in the Sky; sorry, but I gotta pass."

Denise smiled weakly. To be honest, she didn't know much about this "Wizard" guy either. Oh sure, everyone in Fayrah had talked about "Imager"—how he loved them and took special interest in their lives. But she'd never seen him. In fact, she hadn't even been allowed to enter his city. So even if he did exist, she *knew* he'd never have anything to do with her—not Denise Wolff, not the Lincoln Elementary All-School-Oddball.

Josh and Denny finally arrived at the shop. They pushed open the door and the bell above it gave a little jingle as they stepped inside.

"Hey, Gramps," Josh called, "we're here."

An older man with thin, graying hair shuffled out from behind a row of secondhand toasters. "Good evenin' to ya, Joshua," he said. "Oh, and ya brought Denny with ya too—what a fine thing."

"Hi, Grandpa," Denise grinned. She always wound up grinning when she talked to the old man. Then, glancing around the shop, she asked, "Did Nathan ever show up?"

"I haven't seen a sign of the boy."

"Great." Denise sighed. That meant she and Josh would have to go without him. Now that they were inside the shop, away from the moonlight, she pulled out the Bloodstone and dropped it back and forth between her hands, the way she always did when she got nervous.

Unfortunately, the bad news had just begun.

"Listen, lad," Grandpa said to Josh. "I won't be needin' you to close the shop tonight like I thought."

"No?"

"They released Mrs. Thomas from the hospital this afternoon, so I won't be goin' to visit."

Denise spun to Josh in concern, but Josh didn't notice. All he said was, "OK, no problem."

But it *was* a problem! A *BIG* problem! How could she signal for the Fayrahnians to come with Grandpa right there in the store? The creatures barely missed giving the old guy a heart attack the last time they popped in. What would stop it from happening this time?

Terrific, Denise thought. *First, no Nathan, and now no Fayrahnians. What else can go wrong?*

She was about to find out.

Even though she was inside the shop, and was careful to stay away from the windows, Denise had made one little mistake. When she pulled the Bloodstone out of her pocket and nervously fiddled with it, she hadn't noticed the reflection on the pots and pans in the display window. She hadn't noticed the glint of moonlight that hit the side of one of the pots and reflected in her direction. She hadn't noticed that for the briefest second that single glint of moonlight had struck the Bloodstone.

That is, until the rock in her hands started to glow . . .

— CHAPTER TWO —

JUST LIKE OLD TIMES . . . SORTA

First Denny tried to stuff the rock back into her coat pocket. But her pocket began to glow.

Next she sidled up to one of the drawers behind the counter. When no one was looking, she yanked it open, dumped the rock in, and slammed the drawer shut. But pretty soon the drawer began to glow.

Things were not looking good, not at all. She leaned against the drawer in an effort to cover up the glow with her body. At the same time she tried her best to get Joshua's attention. If she could just get him to take Grandpa out of the room for a minute. Forget "a minute," she'd be happy for 15 seconds. But, no. He was too busy with some stupid conversation about sports or school or something. *Figures*, she thought. *He stands around having a good ol' time while I'm over here trying to save his grandfather from the biggest heart attack of all time.*

She began to whistle. Not a bad plan—get Josh's attention and appear to be casual at the same time. The only problem was Denny didn't know beans about whistling. Never had. So instead of a casual little tune, the only sounds that came out of her mouth were wet, puckering wheezes.

She tried drumming her fingers on the counter. Maybe that would get his attention.

Then again, maybe not.

By now the entire top of the counter was beginning to glow. So she did what any intelligent kid would do— she hopped up on the counter and tried to hide the light with her body. First she sat this way, then that. But the light kept spreading, until she had to lie down and completely stretch out across the top of the counter.

So there she was—sprawled out on the counter, noisily drumming her fingers, and at the same time puckering and wheezing away with her pathetic whistle.

Then it happened. It was fainter than usual, but there was no mistaking the clear . . .

BEEP . . .
   BOP . . .
      BURP . . .
         BLEEP . . .

. . . sound of Listro Q's Cross-Dimensionalizer. She'd been expecting that sound. What she didn't expect was the crashing and banging that followed—a crashing and banging that came from out back in the alley.

"What on earth!" Grandpa exclaimed.

"Prowlers?" Joshua asked.

"We'll see about that," Grandpa said as he turned to the counter for his night stick. It was only then that he spotted Denise. By now the glow had completely

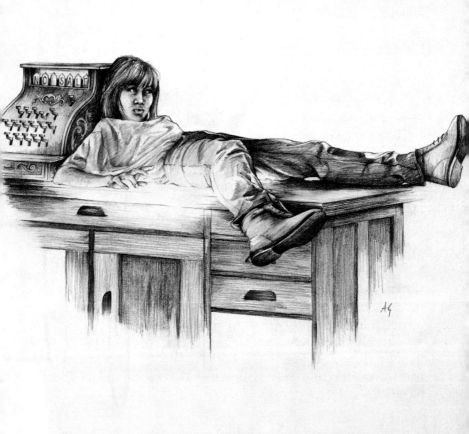

vanished, but she was still lying on the counter. "And would you mind tellin' me what you're up to, girl?" he asked.

"Oh!" She quickly sat up. "I was, uh . . . tired. Yeah, I was tired and thought I'd uh . . ." she faked a little yawn, "you know, get some rest."

Josh and Grandpa looked at each other. Neither was buying the lie, but before they could question her further there was more banging, followed by voices—arguing voices.

Grabbing his night stick from under the counter, Grandpa turned and headed for the back. "Who's out there?" he shouted. "I said, who's out there? What's going on?"

"Stop him!" Denise whispered to Josh.

"What?"

"Those are the Fayrahnians—I'm sure of it."

For a moment Joshua just stared at her.

By now Grandpa had thrown open the back door. "What are you—" but his yell froze mid-sentence.

"We've got to stop him," Denise cried as she hopped off the counter and started for the back.

But Joshua didn't follow.

"Josh?. . ."

The boy still didn't budge. In fact he wasn't moving at all. He just kept staring straight ahead.

"Joshua?"

No response.

She crossed back toward him. "Joshua, what's wrong? Joshua, can you hear me?!"

But the boy didn't move a muscle. Not an eyelid. It was as if he had been suddenly frozen. She took a step or two closer and waved her hand in front of his face. Nothing.

JUST LIKE OLD TIMES...SORTA

It ain't our wish,
the wrong way to be rubbin'.
But we ain't used to welcomes,
with yellin's and clubbin's.

Denise immediately recognized the voice and the awful poetry. "Aristophenix!" she shouted as she spun around to see the furry bear-like creature complete with walking stick and checkered vest. Behind him stood Listro Q, just as tall and cool and purple as always.

Without another word she raced to them and gave them each a hug, but for only a second.

"Whew," she said, quickly pulling away. "What's that smell?"

Aristophenix rolled his eyes over to Listro Q.

The cool purple dude glanced to the floor, cleared his throat and finally replied. His speech was as scrambled and backwards as ever. "Trouble still a little, with Cross-Dimensionalizer have I."

"So?" Denise asked, wondering what that had to do with the smell.

So the wrong coordinates,
he entered again.
So instead of this room,
it's the garbage bin we landed in.

Denise burst out laughing. She wasn't sure which was worse—Listro Q's sense of direction or Aristophenix's awful rhymes. Maybe it was a tie. "But Samson—" she looked around for her favorite of the group—the cute little bug with the glowing red tail. "Where's Samson?"

The little guy got married
to a sweet thing that's dear.
And in Fayrah after weddings,
you don't work for a year.

"That's great!" Denise exclaimed. "So Sammy got married, that's terrific!" She tried her best to sound convincing, but didn't quite pull it off. She had really gotten to love the little guy during their last journey together. The fact that their personalities were exactly alike might have had a little to do with it. And now they were saying he was married? Denise was really happy for him. Well, at least part of her was. But another part felt a little sad and even a little left out.

Speaking of "left out," she suddenly remembered Joshua and spun back to him. "Is he going to be all right?" she asked. "I mean, just standing around frozen like that?"

He and his Grandpa
are a doin' jus' fine.
We've accelerated our clocks,
past the speed of their time.

"What?" Denise didn't quite catch his drift.

"Pot grab there," Listro Q said, pointing to the teapot that sat on the shelf behind her.

She obeyed.

"Drop now it."

Denise looked at him a moment, not sure she understood. He nodded for her to go ahead. So with a shrug she let the teapot drop. But it didn't drop. It just hung there in mid-air.

"How're you doing that?" she asked in amazement. "How're you making it float?"

It ain't floatin' atall,
quite factually, it's fallin'.
We're just speedin' so fast,
that by our time it's crawlin'.

"No kidding," Denise said, grabbing the teapot and

letting it go again. The results were exactly the same. It just hung there. "So Grandpa and Josh aren't frozen. We're just all kinda like . . . moving faster than they are?"

"Correct are you," Listro Q answered.

"But I wanted Josh to come with us," Denise protested. "He doesn't believe in any of this stuff, and I wanted him to come see for—"

Aristophenix politely interrupted:

We understand the problem;
we've been to the Weaver.
When it comes to Imager,
Josh ain't no believer.

Denise nodded. That was it in a nutshell. She wasn't sure what they meant by the "Weaver," but they were right on the button about Josh refusing to believe.

"Worry not to," Listro Q assured her. "With us, coming he will be." Then, with a smile, he added, "But not all that's."

Denise waited for more.

"Problem, says Weaver, still *you* have."

"Me?"

"By Imager, how loved you are," Listro Q continued, "still, understand you do not."

Denise opened her mouth to argue but quickly closed it. It wouldn't do any good. Whoever this Weaver guy was, he had her figured out almost as well as Josh. It was true. When it came to Imager, Denny knew there had to be somebody out there running the show. After all she'd seen and heard on her last trip, she knew that much. But for the Imager to actually *like* her, to take a personal interest in her, when he was so awesome and powerful and stuff; well, if you asked her, it sounded like a lot of wishful thinking—a nice idea, but definitely fantasyland.

Still, according to Listro Q, this was the other reason they'd come—to prove to her that it wasn't fantasy.

So pack up yer bags;
let's get ready to shove.
For Josh it's the proof,
for you it's the love.

"What about Nathan?" Denise suddenly remembered. "He wanted to come, too."

"Later come he can. But now move must we."

Denise hesitated another second before finally giving Listro Q a nod. Without a word he reached for the little remote control box, pressed four buttons . . .

BEEP . . .
   BOP . . .
      BURP . . .
         BLEEP . . .

. . . and they were off.

Suddenly the room was flooded with a blinding light. And then, just as suddenly, there was no room at all— just the bright whiteness. As with their last trip, Denise felt herself falling. Once again she looked around and saw thousands of bright, multi-colored lights—all falling toward a much brighter brightness below—toward The Center, toward Imager's home.

It took awhile for her eyes to adjust to the brightness. But at last she was able to make out the glowing forms of Aristophenix and Listro Q beside her. They were quietly speaking to Joshua—at least she thought it was Joshua. But this Joshua was bigger and more powerful— especially his upper body. He had to be, because in each of his thick, muscular arms he carried a huge clay pot, filled to the brim with water—but not the water of earth. It was the water from Fayrah's Stream, the water that was actually made up of liquid letters and words.

"So, you're finally with us," Josh said, grinning at Denise. But he really wasn't *speaking*—it was more like he was *thinking*.

"What do you mean?" she thought back.

"Speeded up time his did we, past yours," Listro Q explained. "To tell him everything, so frightened not he'd be."

Denny nodded, not all that thrilled with the idea. It was one thing to zip around somebody else who was frozen. But to be the one who was frozen, well now that was different. Who knew what kind of idiotic expression she'd had stuck on her face, or for how long it'd been stuck there?

"Don't worry," Josh thought back to her as if he'd read her mind. "You looked incredible . . . you still do!"

Denise shot him an angry look. It wasn't like Josh to be mean. But when she saw his eyes she realized he wasn't. Instead, he was looking at her with a kind of . . . well, the only word she could think of was—*admiration*.

A little flustered and caught off-guard, Denny looked down at herself and immediately saw the reason for Joshua's comment. Once again she was wearing the gorgeous Wedding Gown—the gown she had seen in the Stream, the one made of intricate lace and tiny glowing pearls. But the pearls weren't all that was glowing. She could feel the color rising to her cheeks. It was an amazing fact, but she had actually been complimented over her looks. And, worse yet, she was actually blushing over it!

Not sure of what to say or do, she avoided the topic all together. Turning to the Fayrahnians she asked, "Did you guys tell him about The Center? Did you tell him what he has to do to cross Interface?"

But neither Listro Q or Aristophenix answered. Their eyes were already closed and their heads were tilted back. They were quietly beginning to speak words of love and appreciation for Imager.

"Yeah, they told me," Joshua volunteered. "I'm supposed to think of happy stuff, maybe sing a song."

"More than that," Denise said, almost too urgently. Suddenly memories of the last time she tried to enter The Center flooded her mind. Awful, terrifying memories. Memories of being flung into an empty darkness. "You've got to sing one of your Grandpa's songs. That's what Nathan did. The only way he made it through was by singing one of your grandpa's old Irish hymns."

A look of concern crossed Josh's face. "A hymn?"

Denise nodded and looked down. The Center was quickly approaching. Already she could make out the bright glowing buildings. Already she could see the thin layer of fog that formed the subtle but impenetrable barrier—the fog called *Interface*.

"I don't know, Denny. I don't remember any hymns."

Denise felt a brief wave of panic, and with the panic came the first vibrations. They were faint, but they rapidly increased.

"Sure you do," she insisted, trying to push back the fear. "He used to sing them to you guys at bedtime."

"A hymn? I don't think . . ."

The vibrating was getting worse, more like shaking, and it grew more violent by the second.

"Come on, Joshua!" she called. There was no mistaking the fear in her voice now. "You can remember!"

The scowl on Josh's face grew more intense.

Denise cast another look down. They were practically

at Interface. Already the shaking was turning into jarring bounces and teeth-rattling knocks. Any moment, they would enter the fog where the bouncing would increase a thousand times, where it would turn to violent lurchings and lungings. But that would only last a second. Before they knew it they would be yanked to a screeching halt—then, without warning, they would be hurdled in the opposite direction, back past the Secondhand Shop and out into the empty, black void—an empty blackness full of nothing but fear and more blackness.

"Come on, Joshua! THINK!" Denise shouted. She would not experience the terror of that darkness again— she *could not*. "COME ON . . . THINK! *THINK!!!*"

The tossings and bangings were nightmarish—like a carnival ride out of control, and growing worse. Then she heard it. It was slow and halting at first, but it quickly grew in volume and confidence.

"Be Thou . . . my vision, O Lord . . . of my . . . heart . . ." Josh was singing. Sometimes there were long pauses, as if the words were just beyond his memory. Then he would hum. But regardless, one way or the other he pressed on . . .

"Naught be all else . . . mm-mm-mmmmm that Thou art."

"That's it, Josh!" Denise cried. "Keep it up! Keep it up!"

"Thou my best thought . . . by day or by night.

"Mmm-mm mmm mm-mm, Thy presence my light."

The shaking started to decrease, and just in time. Almost immediately they dropped into the first wispy layers of Interface. Denise closed her eyes and forced herself to concentrate on the words. Eventually she tried to sing along—half singing, half humming, as Josh continued . . .

"Be Thou my Wisdom, mm-mm my true Word,
Mm mm-mm mmm mmm and Thou with me, Lord."
The shaking continued to decrease.
"Thou my great Father, and I Thy true son.
Thou in me dwelleth, and I with Thee one."

Finally the shaking stopped altogether. They had passed through Interface—Denise knew it. Even with her eyes closed, she could tell everything was much brighter now—*much* brighter. She was tempted to open her eyes, but didn't dare. She knew the sight would fill her with fear—and with the fear the awful shaking would return.

Then she felt the firm pressure of something under her feet. They had landed! At The Center!

Denise was still afraid to open her eyes—afraid of what she might see. But she also knew she'd hate herself forever if she didn't take a look . . . just one little peek.

— Chapter Three —

Arrivals

As Denise and the guys landed at The Center, a welcoming party just five dimensions away was also preparing for her arrival.

"Click clickCLICK   CLICKclick
      CLICKCLICKclick   click   CLICKclick."

It was the Vice-governor of Biiq. He was at his banqueting table giving orders to Bud, one of the greatest scientists in his realm. Nearly 150 epochs had passed since they'd quit using words in this Kingdom. Words were so inaccurate when it came to real communication. And in Biiq, the Land of Math and Science, accuracy was supreme. So, instead of words, everyone simply clicked their tongues. The pauses between clicks, the number of clicks, and the loudness of each click said it all, and said it far more accurately than anything as old-fashioned as words. Of course it made their poetry a little difficult to grasp, but, hey, they were scientists. What did they care about rhyme or verse?

The information had just arrived from the Weaver. Biiq would soon be receiving two precious Threads from the Upside-down Kingdom. One Thread knew Imager, but couldn't understand his love. The other refused to believe in him at all, because, as he said, "It goes against the laws of logic and science."

The argument made Bud chuckle. It was *because* of Imager's infinite logic and his awesome scientific properties that Biiq was created in the first place. Here, people could spend their whole lives exploring Imager—understanding him through mathematical formulas, marveling over him through scientific investigation. Here, people could experience and explain Imager more deeply than anyplace else in the Universe! Of course the boys over in the art Kingdoms might not entirely agree, but who cared? Today, *they* were the ones chosen to help the Upside-Downers understand. *They* were the ones given the privilege of making Imager more real to them.

For several epochs, Bud had been in charge of building the special laboratory called the "Machine." Throughout that time, rumors had spread far and wide regarding who or what the Machine was for and when it would be used. Well, today, those rumors would finally be put to rest. The Machine was designed for the two Upside-Downers, particularly for the one who didn't understand Imager's love. And, today, the Vice-governor was giving Bud orders to welcome them to his Kingdom, and to introduce them to the wonderful invention.

Bud received the orders with an enthusiastic, "CLICKclick click   CLICK   clickCLICK," then turned and immediately fell over the nearest chair. Now that wouldn't have been a problem. People around the

Palace were accustomed to Bud's being a little—how shall we say it?—*heavy on his feet*. But when he jumped up, stepped on the Vice-governor's sleeping cat, knocked down the waiter carrying the Vice-governor's main course, then spun around, tripped, and landed face-first in the Vice-governor's cream of celery soup, well, it was bordering on being a problem.

The Vice-governor stared down at Bud and pursed his lips in self-control.

Bud stared up from the soup bowl and tried to smile. Then, without a word, he rose, wrung out his mustache, gave a weak sort of salute, and ran out of the Palace for all he was worth. He really wasn't embarrassed. Such catastrophes were normal for him—too normal. He may be Biiq's greatest scientist, but he was also Biiq's biggest clod.

But none of that mattered now. After all these years of preparing the Machine, he'd finally be able to show the rest of the Kingdom his true stuff. He'd have to hurry, though—the Upside-Downers were only making a brief stop at The Center. Since neither of them were re-Breathed, they couldn't stay there long. Imager's presence would destroy them. So Bud raced off as fast as he could. There was so much to prepare and so little time to prepare it.

———

Denise's first impression of The Center was the blinding white light. By now, she was getting pretty used to that. What really caught her attention was the singing. And by singing we're not talking your average, run-of-the-mill church choir stuff. We're talking swelling, breathtaking, send-shivers-up-your-spine type singing. In fact, it was so beautiful and awe-inspiring that before she knew it, a lump had formed in her throat.

At first Denise thought the song came from the various light-forms that strolled past her. But once her eyes grew accustomed to the city's brilliance, she saw that the singing didn't only come from these light-creatures. It came from everywhere—the buildings, the streets, the trees, even the blades of grass (a neat trick, since none of these things had a mouth). Still, somehow, some way, they all seemed to be singing.

But that was just one of the ways the song was different. Another was that Denny didn't only hear it. She could feel it inside her. That's right. Somehow the notes did more than enter her ears. They seeped into her whole being, vibrating her muscles, her bones. It was as if her very insides were starting to sing the song.

Aristophenix grinned at the puzzled look that crossed Denise's face and explained:

> Everything of Imager
> vibrates with his Voice.
> From stars to dirt clods,
> all sing and rejoice.

Denise nodded, pretending to understand. But before she really caught on, something even stranger happened. Tears. Tears began to flow down her cheeks, and for once she didn't try to stop them. Suddenly all she wanted to do was sit down on the glowing street and have a good cry. Not a cry of sadness, but a cry of joy. Imagine, Denise Tougher-Than-Nails Wolff, wanting to sit on the ground and cry for joy! Amazing!

She couldn't put her finger on it, but she suspected the emotions had something to do with the song. Because as she felt herself joining in, she also felt something else. For the very first time in her life, Denny began to feel that she *belonged*. It was an incredible feeling. But somehow, after all her years of searching and trying to fit in, Denise felt she was finally—well the word that kept coming to her mind was "home." Denny finally felt that she was *home*!

She glanced over to Josh beside her. He was crying, too. Good, that meant she wasn't totally out of her mind. Or was she? Because now she noticed something even stranger. She could see *through* him! Not clearly, mind you. It was more like looking at a stained-glass window. Josh's form and coloring were still there, along with most of his details. But now she could actually see some of the light-creatures moving behind him!

She raised her arm and looked at her own hand. Same thing. *Oh, brother,* she thought, *now what's going on?* She looked to Aristophenix for an answer but it was Listro Q's turn to explain.

"Super Reality, The Center is. Everything else of this, shadow is."

Denise looked at her hand again. He was right. Because she wasn't glowing like the rest of The Center, and because she seemed to be transparent, she looked like— well, the weird thing was she really *did* look like a shadow.

The thought didn't exactly thrill her, but it didn't depress her either. Not here. Not with all this joy and goodness and wonder.

She glanced back up to the passing light-creatures. Whenever she looked straight at them, all she saw was a blazing glare of light. But when she looked away, and caught them out of the corner of her eye, she could make out some of their details. Details that showed her these little creatures really weren't creatures at all.

A good example was the light approaching her now.

How could it be living? A sidelong glance revealed it was only a hammock—that's right, a swinging hammock. But not just any old swinging hammock. It was the very hammock that hung in her grandfather's apple orchard! She was certain of it. It was the very same hammock that she, her mother, and dad, used to romp and play in—the same one that held all those wonderful memories of their times together . . . back when they *were* together.

As it passed by her, Denise tried to see who was in it, but without success. Every time she focused on a detail, the whole thing blurred back into a glare of brightness.

Then there were the sounds—laughing, giggling, shouting. Unmistakably the voices of her parents and herself. In fact, for a moment Denise actually felt like she were back in that hammock, nestled securely within her parents' loving arms.

The joy was impossible to describe. She looked to Aristophenix for another explanation. He smiled and answered:

Reality of The Center,
your logical mind cannot grasp.
So your brain sees in symbols,
to help lighten the task.

It was tough to find her voice with all the emotion rising in her throat, but at last Denise was able to speak. "You mean, that's not my grandpa's hammock?"

"A hammock?" Aristophenix chuckled slightly. "Ask Joshua."

"No way," Josh whispered in awe as he watched the same light-creature pass. "That's my whole Little League baseball team back in fifth grade—back when we won the All-City Championship."

"Right," she joked. "Your whole Little League baseball team." But at a glance she could see he wasn't joking. In fact, his face was glowing with as much wonder and joy as hers. It was incredible. He saw the light-creature as one thing and she saw it as something entirely different. But whatever they saw, it made them feel exactly the same—wonderfully warm, incredibly happy.

She turned back toward the hammock—or Little League team, whatever it was. Now it was farther down the road, and looked like all the other glowing lights. Any detail was swallowed up in the overall glare. But it wasn't just the glare of the light-creature. It was also the glare of the horizon.

For just over the nearby ridge, past the hammock, was a light so radiant, so brilliant that it made the back of Denise's eyes ache. And it made all of the other lights of The Center dim by comparison.

But it was more than just light. There was something different about it. It had a quality, a kind of *splendor* about it, a kind of *glory*. A glory so intense that it forced Denny to catch her breath in astonishment.

Excitement started to pound against her ribs. She began to breathe faster, harder. No one had to tell her. She knew who the singing was for—and she knew where the glory was from. She knew that just over that ridge was the source of all The Center's light, all The Center's goodness. She knew that just over that ridge she would finally find . . . Imager.

Without a word she turned and started toward the ridge.

Both Aristophenix and Listro Q spotted her and cried out in alarm, "NO! DENNY, DON'T!"

But Denise barely heard them. She picked up her pace, breaking from a walk to a run.

Listro Q took off after her. "Denny! No! Back here come!"

But Denny wasn't listening. All she could do was stare at the light blazing from behind the ridge. It burned into her eyes, but she could not stop looking. Faster and faster she ran.

It took more than a little doing, but at last Listro Q finally was able to catch up. "Denny," he shouted, running beside her, "stop you at once!"

"Why?" she puffed, refusing to take her eyes off the approaching ridge.

"As close this is, dare get as you!"

"Why?" she repeated, still not looking at him, still running for all she was worth.

"Re-Breathed not you are. Destroy you his Presence will."

If Denise had any air in her lungs to spare she would have broken out laughing. "No way!" she panted. "I feel his love now. I finally see what you and Aristophenix have been talking about."

"But, yes . . ." Listro Q was getting desperate. "Unapproachable is he, too pure for you he is!"

By now they were passing the other light-creatures that were heading toward the ridge; first the hammock, and then one creature after another as Denny continued to push on.

They were nearly at the top. Imager was nearly in view.

The music was much louder now. Denny's joy was so ecstatic she could barely concentrate. The song was everywhere—inside her, overpowering her, consuming her.

And the light. It was so bright that it was all she could see. It was all she wanted to see. It was all that mattered.

If Listro Q was still shouting at her, she couldn't hear him. If her feet were still touching the ground, she couldn't feel them. There was only the light.

But something more frightening was happening. Without even knowing it, Denise's thoughts had started to dissolve. One memory after another began to slip away. In fact, if someone had asked Denny her name she wouldn't have remembered it. At that moment she had no name. Her thoughts, her memories, her very identity were disappearing.

But it wasn't only her identity. It was also her body. Her very body was becoming transparent; it was also disappearing!

Vanishing memories! Vanishing thoughts! Vanishing body! Everything about Denise was starting to vanish! We're not just talking about becoming invisible. We're talking about *everything* disappearing. With every step Denise took toward the light, she existed less and less!

This was the horror Listro Q had tried to warn her of. By approaching the unapproachable light, Denise was ceasing to exist!

"DENNY! ME TO LISTEN!!" Listro Q cried. But it did no good.

Then the unthinkable happened. Denise ran straight through one of the light-creatures. She had become so unreal that she was able to pass through solid objects. It was as if she were only a vapor; as if she weren't there. And for good reason: she *wasn't* there . . . well, at least most of her wasn't there. And after a few more steps, she wouldn't be there at all.

At last, in desperation, Listro Q took a flying leap toward Denny. He hit her hard at the waist, wrapped his arms around her, and began to drag her down for the tackle.

But to his dismay, he crashed to the ground alone. Her body had passed right through his arms as if it were vapor.

"DENNY!!!!!" he cried.

But Denny no longer heard him. She no longer cared. For all intents and purposes, Denny no longer existed.

— CHAPTER FOUR —

THE WEAVER

"Nine hours!" Josh complained as he rose to his feet and began pacing the room. "How much longer?" He glanced toward the doors that had been tightly shut ever since an emergency team raced through them with the last remaining vapors of Denise.

For the past several hours Josh had been eyeing those doors, studying the stark, black lettering that read:

RESTRICTED AREA
ENTRANCE PROHIBITED

But Josh knew that *restricted* or not, he was going to have to break through those doors to find his friend. It was just a matter of time, and of getting past the two huge, elk-like guards that blocked the doors with their antlers.

Aristophenix stood at one of the windows on the

other side of the marbled room. Listro Q was nearby. They were in Fayrah now. Listro Q had cross-dimensionalized them over as quickly as possible. And since Josh was an Upside-Downer, Aristophenix had already given him the water from the Stream so he could see and hear right-side up.

Now the pudgy, bear-like creature gazed out onto the lush courtyard where a hundred Fayrahnians quietly waited . . . and prayed. Denise had been their friend. In fact, many of them had been rescued as a result of her last visit.

Aristophenix raised his eyes from the crowd to the distant Blood Mountains. They glowed and pulsed the way they always did when citizens of the Upside-down Kingdom were present. "I shouldn't have taken ya there," he sighed heavily. There was no trace of poetry in his voice. Normally that might have been a relief, except that Aristophenix only forgot his poetry when things looked their worst. "Until you were both re-Breathed," he repeated, "I shouldn't have taken ya there."

Suddenly the door leading to the courtyard flew open. Two Fayrahnians raced in. One looked exactly like Aristophenix—except for the four ears and two noses. The other looked like a seahorse with legs. They were holding a long, hollow tube between them. Something glowed inside it.

"More Threads from The Center!" Seahorse cried. Immediately the Elk Guards stepped aside as the sealed doors whisked open.

It was now or never.

In a flash Josh made his move.

"Joshua!" Aristophenix called.

But it was too late. Josh broke past the guards and

raced down the glaring white hallway as fast as he could.

"Stop him—Stop him at once!" Seahorse shouted. "He must not see her tapestry!"

The two guards galloped down the hallway after him—the sound of their hooves echoing against the marble walls.

Josh glanced over his shoulder. They were quickly gaining on him. He was no match for their powerful legs.

But he continued to run. He wasn't worried about being hit or hurt; he knew that wasn't the Fayrahnian way. He *was* worried about getting through the opening up ahead before the Elks could leap over him and block his path with their giant antlers.

Behind them were Listro Q and the other two Fayrahnians carrying the glowing tube. And behind them, as always, was Aristophenix bringing up the rear—his roly-poly little body doing its best to catch up.

The opening was just a few feet ahead. Josh bore down, straining with every muscle. Suddenly the clatter of hooves stopped. He knew the Elk Guards had leaped into the air and were now sailing over his head. He knew that any second they'd land in front of him and prevent his rescue.

Josh had no choice—he did what any ex-All-City Little League champion would do. He thrust his feet out, leaned his body back and slid across the slick marble floor.

It worked perfectly. Even though the Elks landed in front of him, they weren't able to drop their antlers down in time to block him. Josh slid between their legs and out through the opening.

He leaped to his feet but quickly came to a stop. He was in some sort of giant hall, standing in the balcony overlooking a hundred different creatures—Fayrahni-

ans, who because of his disturbance were all looking right back at him.

Well, all but one.

In the center of the huge room was a single man, hunched over, and concentrating on an old-fashioned loom used for weaving fabric. But the threads were not ordinary threads—they glowed. But not with ordinary light. They glowed with the same brilliance and beauty as the light from The Center. And the pattern the old man was weaving shimmered and sparkled with such depth and beauty that Josh could barely look at it without feeling an ache in the back of his throat.

"Bring him here," the Weaver ordered. He never looked up but kept concentrating on the pattern before him.

"But, Weaver," Seahorse called, "he knows the girl, he must not see."

"It is too late, yes it is," the Weaver answered matter-of-factly. "Bring him here."

The Elk Guards exchanged nervous glances. Apparently, approaching the Weaver when he was working was not their idea of a good time. But they didn't have to worry. At that exact moment, Aristophenix waddled out of the hallway, puffing up a storm.

The error was (pant, pant) all mine,
to this (pant) I confess.
I'll take him (pant, pant) below
to (pant) clear up all of this mess.

The guards didn't have to be asked twice. Gratefully, they stepped aside.

Gasping with every step, Aristophenix came forward and took Josh's arm. Well, to some it looked like he took hold of it. To most it looked like it was Josh who was doing the holding as he did his best to steady the exhausted bear. With a deep breath for courage, Aristophenix turned to lead Josh down the stairs toward the Weaver. But to everyone's surprise, Listro Q suddenly stepped forward to join him.

Aristophenix spoke in a hushed whisper:

What are ya doin'?
Don't be a sap.
As the leader, it's me
who should be takin' the rap.

But Listro Q only smiled. "Cool" was all he said.

Try as he might, Aristophenix couldn't help but smile back. Listro Q *was* cool. Cool and loyal. Loyal to the end.

But Josh wasn't concerned with Listro Q's loyalty right now. He was thinking of his own loyalty. Denise was down there somewhere. And he knew he had to help her. But where was she? Where could she have—

And then he spotted it. Far from the Weaver, on the other side of the room, on a table beneath intense, glaring lights, was the faintest outline of a human body.

"Denny!" Josh gasped.

"Correct," Listro Q whispered as they started to move down the steps.

"But . . . why isn't anybody with her?" Josh demanded. "They're all with the Weaver, when they should be at the other table trying to save Denise!"

Listro Q tried to explain. "Physical body of hers only on that table is," he said, pointing to the table where Denise's remains lay. "But her *character*," he said, pointing to the Weaver and his loom, "her character over there is."

"What are you talking about?" Josh snapped. He motioned toward the glowing pattern on the Weaver's loom.

"That's just some stupid design he's making."

Aristophenix patiently explained:

That design is her life.
Each fiber and strand
is woven together,
as Imager planned.

Josh just stared at him. He knew his mouth was hanging open but he didn't much care. "You mean, *that* . . ." He pointed at the design on the loom. "*That's* her life—that pattern is who she is?"

Aristophenix smiled and nodded.

Each thread is a moment
in her life's Master Plan.
To create a character
both glorious and grand.

Josh continued to stare at the loom and at the pattern that was forming. Aristophenix was right. It *was* glorious. It *was* grand. No wonder he was so choked up when he first saw it. But there was something else . . .

The more Josh stared at the pattern, the more it began to make sense. Somehow the design really was Denise. Oh, not her body, not what she looked like on the outside—but how she was on the inside. Her character, her personality—somehow the pattern that appeared on the loom was what Denise was like as a *person*.

Then Josh saw something else. "Wait a minute!" he called in alarm, "What's that?"

The Weaver had picked up a dark, ugly thread and was adding it to the pattern. It was an awful, sinister color; so evil that it sent a chill down Josh's back. Such ugly darkness had no place with such beauty. In fact, it looked to Josh like the Weaver was about to destroy his wonderful work by adding the strange thread.

"What are you doing?" Josh shouted. By now they had reached the bottom of the steps. They were only a few yards from the loom. "Stop it! You're ruining it!"

Everyone tensed as Josh's voice echoed around the room—everyone but the Weaver. For a moment the old man didn't answer, but remained hunched over the loom, carefully working in the dark, ominous thread. When he did speak, it was only a sentence, and he never looked up.

"This thread will give her strength and depth, yes it will."

Josh barely heard him. He couldn't take his eyes off the thread. It was hideous. If this pattern, this tapestry really was Denny's life, that thread would bring her incredible pain, incredible heartache. Even now, as the Weaver continued to work it into the pattern, it seemed to drain all the beauty and color from the other threads, ruining the entire design.

"Stop it! You're hurting her! You're . . . you're . . ."

But the Weaver kept on working.

Joshua had to help. He couldn't just stand around and let the old man destroy his friend's life. Without a moment's hesitation, he pulled his arm away from Aristophenix, and started for the loom. He'd tear the awful thread out of the Weaver's hand if he had to!

But the surrounding Fayrahnians quickly moved in to block his path. He tried to push and shove his way through, but there were just too many of them. If he managed to force one aside three more appeared in its place.

Desperately he looked around. There had to be something he could do. *Wait a minute! What about Denny's body? Her physical form on the brightly lit table across the room!* There wasn't much of her there—just a faint outline. And of course it was only the outside of her, without her personality. But hey, some of Denise was better than none of her!

Listro Q was the first to see the look in his eyes. "Josh—No!"

But he was too late. The boy raced across the hall. The few Fayrahnians that stood between Josh and the table tried to stop him, but he was too fast and too strong. Those he couldn't sidestep, he shoved out of the way as he sprinted toward the brightly lit table that held the faint, quivering form of Denise's body.

"You don't understand!" Aristophenix shouted. "You'll cripple her character! You'll ruin her!"

For the first time the Weaver glanced up. And for the first time a look of concern crossed his face. But it lasted only a second. He quickly returned to his task, working faster than ever.

Josh was getting closer. Just another twenty feet or so, and a few more Fayrahnians. And then what? He wasn't sure. Maybe he'd scoop the faint outline of Denise's body into his arms and try to escape with it. Anything to get her away from the Weaver and his awful dark thread.

But across the room the Weaver worked faster still, his nimble fingers moving the dark thread in and out of the strands, working it in as quickly as possible. It had become a race. The Weaver desperate to complete his task; Josh desperate to save Denise before he did.

A Fayrahnian reached out and nearly had Josh, until the boy faked a left and expertly spun away to the right. Besides being a base stealer, Josh was also a pretty good halfback.

Now it was a clear shot to Denise.

That is, until Seahorse leaped off the high balcony

and landed between them. The poor guy had obviously seen too many super-hero movies and figured this was his big break. Unfortunately, as he landed on the hard floor, something else broke instead. He grabbed his ankle and began writhing around, screaming in agony. (Sea-horses have never been much for handling pain.)

Josh sidestepped the poor creature and continued to race for the table. Now there was absolutely nothing between him and the quivering form of Denise's body.

The Weaver had just six strands to go—six strands through which to weave the dark thread, making it a permanent part of Denise's tapestry. *In and out. In and out.* Beads of perspiration appeared on his forehead.

Josh was nearly there. Just a few more steps.

In and out. In and out.

The boy continued forward. Now he raised his arms toward Denise. She was nearly in his grasp.

"JOSHUA, NO!" Listro Q shouted. "COMPLETE FIRST SHE MUST BE!"

But he paid no attention.

In and out.

And then, as Josh's hands touched her semi-trans-parent form . . .

In and out. The Weaver was finished! The dark thread was permanently in place!

Suddenly the quivering, transparent image of Denise took shape—she had substance—she had weight. Just as Josh wrapped his arms around her and scooped her up.

"Denny!" he cried.

"Joshua . . ." she gasped.

The Weaver sighed deeply and leaned back in his chair. Removing his spectacles, he grabbed a handker-chief and blotted the perspiration from his face. It was close—too close. Joshua had nearly beaten him. But at the very last second he had managed to complete the weaving, to complete Denise.

All that was left were the explanations, and preparations for their upcoming trip to Biiq. The Weaver wished they'd start listening more instead of being so bullheaded. But then what could he expect? After all, they were from the Upside-down Kingdom.

"Upside-Downers," he sighed. "What a curious lot. Yes they are."

CHAPTER FIVE

A GUIDED TOUR

"Let me get this straight." Josh scowled. "You mean to tell me that you've woven the pattern of every person that's ever lived?"

"That's right, yes it is . . . and that ever will," the Weaver added.

Josh's scowl deepened as they walked through a series of large, cavernous hallways. On each wall hung hundreds of shimmering tapestries. Each was intricately beautiful, magnificently breathtaking. And each was fashioned from the same glowing threads as Denise's pattern. The whole place was like a giant art museum. But not like those that are full of dull, boring, masterpieces—the ones they drag you through on school field trips. No way! These tapestries were full of life—glowing, shimmering, quivering-with-beauty life—The Center's life.

It had been several hours since Denise was revived. Now she walked between Josh and the Weaver as the old man did his best to fill them in on all that had happened.

"How do you keep up?" Denise asked. "I mean, weaving so many people? Where do you find the time?"

"Eternity lasts awhile," the Weaver chuckled. "We had a bit of a head-start on you."

Josh was still having a difficult time understanding. "I'm sorry," he apologized. "This is just a little too weird. I don't think I can buy all of it."

The Weaver gave another chuckle. "I knew that would be a problem, yes I did. When Imager first asked me to weave that thread into you, I knew you'd have a hard time."

"What thread?"

"The logic thread—the one always wanting proof."

Josh and Denise exchanged looks. Well, whoever this old timer was, he certainly had Josh figured out.

"But that's OK." The old man smiled as they shuffled out of one hall and into another. "That's part of the plan, yes it is. That's why your tapestry is in these most honored halls."

"You're kidding!" Josh exclaimed, then immediately caught himself. As a scientist he should sound more grownup and *logical*, not so childish and excited. He continued, this time forcing his voice to stay low and calm. "That is to say, my tapestry is here?"

"Of course." The Weaver laughed.

"Well, can I, you know—is it possible to see it?"

"Yeah!" Denise joined in.

"Sorry, that's out of the question. Yes it is."

"Why?"

"An Upside-Downer is never pleased with his pattern. No he isn't. Until his thread, or his design is added to the Imager's Final Tapestry he always tries to change it."

"I wouldn't do that—I promise." Again Josh grimaced at the urgency in his voice.

"You wouldn't, you say?"

"No, you can trust me."

"Just as I could trust you not to change Denise's tapestry?"

"You saw my tapestry?" Denise asked in astonishment.

Josh ignored her and answered the Weaver. "Well, that was, you know, different."

"Josh, you saw my tapestry?" Denise persisted.

"How different?" the old man asked.

"You were putting in that ugly, dark thread."

"What thread?" Denise demanded, growing more and more frustrated that she was being ignored.

"But the thread will give her character, yes it will. It will give her—"

"WHAT THREAD ARE YOU GUYS TALKING ABOUT?" Denny's shout echoed in the giant room. She hadn't meant to be quite so loud. All she wanted was some attention. Well, she definitely had it now. For a moment both of them stared at her as if she'd lost her mind. She smiled weakly and repeated the question a bit more quietly. "Uh, what thread are we, you know, talking about here?"

"There is a reappearing thread in your life, yes there is," the Weaver carefully explained. "It is dark and sinister."

"It's really awful," Josh added.

Denise looked first to the Weaver, then to Josh, then back to the Weaver. "Well . . . why? I mean, if it's so dark and bad, why do I have to have it?"

It was the Weaver's turn to hesitate. He hadn't intended to get into all this detail. But Josh had pulled him in and there was no way out but the truth. "The thread will give you character . . . depth," he explained. "It will make you one of Imager's most valued creations. Yes it will."

"But . . . what is it?" Denise coaxed. "What type of darkness is it?"

The Weaver gave her a careful look. But instead of answering, he slowly came to a stop in front of another shimmering masterpiece. "Tell me," he asked, "what do you two think of this tapestry?"

"It's terrific," Denise answered. "Just like all the others but—"

"Take a closer look," he insisted. "Go on, both of you. Step up and look closely at the threads."

The two exchanged glances and obeyed.

"Are they all the same?" the man asked. "The threads, I mean. Are they all the same color and brightness?"

"Of course not," Josh answered. "Otherwise it would be boring; there'd be nothing to it."

The old man smiled at his answer. "I wove you well, Joshua O'Brien." Then, looking back up at the tapestry, he continued, "And the darkest thread, do you see it?"

"Yes, it's right here in the center." Denise pointed. "It runs all the way to the bottom."

"Good. Now step back and see how the one dark thread adds to the overall beauty of the piece."

Once again the two obeyed. And as they stood staring at the pattern, they could see how the one dark thread, woven in and out, created the strength, the very foundation for the rest of the threads. It gave the entire tapestry its depth, its texture, its beauty.

"If I would have disobeyed Imager, if I would have

refused to add that thread—tell me, what would have happened?"

"The whole pattern would fall apart," Denise answered.

Josh agreed. "The tapestry would be nothing without it."

"Right again, yes you are."

"Who is this person?" Josh asked. His suspicions were beginning to grow. "The pattern looks—it looks kinda familiar. Do we know him?"

Denise turned to the Weaver. Now that Josh mentioned it, there was something vaguely familiar about it.

The Weaver broke into a smile. There was no missing the pride in his craftsmanship. "This is your brother— Nathan O'Brien."

Denny and Josh both gasped. It was true. They could see it. Somehow, some way the pattern of the tapestry perfectly captured Nathan's personality. Not just the spoiled, selfish Nathan of a few months ago, but the new, giving Nathan who had begun to emerge. It was amazing—the design really did capture Nathan's character. Completely.

"And the dark thread?" Josh asked.

"The dark thread is Nathan's hip—the deformity that has caused him to limp with such pain over the years."

The two looked at the tapestry again. And again they were amazed.

The Weaver continued, "Look how all the brighter threads radiate from the darker one. Look how they're highlighted—how their beauty is intensified. Without the darker thread, the tapestry would be nothing. It would have none of its profound depth, its extraordinary strength."

Denise and Josh continued to stare. It was true. Nathan's greatest handicap, in the hands of the Weaver, had become his greatest strength. Amazing.

The Weaver finished with one last thought. "Imager has great plans for all of you. But sometimes the heart is not big enough to hold such plans. Sometimes it must be enlarged through hardship."

The silence lasted several moments. Finally Josh turned to the Weaver. "But . . . but what about Denny's question? You never answered it. What about *her* thread?"

The Weaver looked curiously at Josh. "I'd forgotten your persistence. Perhaps I wove you too well."

But Josh wouldn't back down. He wanted an answer and an answer he would get.

With a deep sigh the Weaver explained. "Denny first met that thread in Keygarp. She saw it circling high above her in the frozen forest."

Denise could only stare at him. The hair on her arms began to rise.

"Since then she has also seen it in her dreams." The Weaver turned to Denise. "In fact, the last time you saw it was this afternoon—when you were daydreaming in your sixth period English class."

"The witch?" Denise gasped. She felt like she'd been hit in the stomach. "That thing flying around with those awful black wings?"

"She's not a witch, Denise. No she isn't. She's the Illusionist—a queen, really. That is, until Nathan destroyed her kingdom. In any case, she and the evil Bobok have made a pact. You have been promised to her."

"*Promised* to her!"

The Weaver nodded gravely.

"What are you talking about?" Denise could feel the

tops of her ears getting hot with anger. "Nobody can *promise* me to anyone. What do I look like, a baseball card? People can't just trade me around without my permission."

"That's right," Josh agreed. "Doesn't she have something to say about it?"

"Of course she does. Every decision you make is of your own free will. These threads only show the *final* outcome—what Imager *knows* you will eventually choose."

"And he knows I'm getting sold to some ugly, bat-winged queen?"

"No. He knows that your struggle against her will be fierce."

"So, will I win?"

The Weaver hesitated. Finally he shook his head. "I cannot answer that, no I can't. The decision will be yours."

"But you know what I'll decide, you just said so."

"Please," The Weaver motioned toward the doorway at the end of the hall. "They are waiting."

"Who?"

"Your friends, Listro Q and Aristophenix."

"But, you haven't answered my quest—"

"I have said too much already."

"But—"

He raised his hand for silence. It was a gentle movement but one that made it clear the topic was closed. Starting toward the doorway, he changed the subject altogether. "Your purpose for this journey, has it been fulfilled?"

"What purpose?" Denise asked.

"For Joshua."

"Oh, you mean proving Imager to him?"

The Weaver nodded.

She looked to Josh.

The boy was staring hard at the marble floor. He wanted to be kind. He knew a lot of people had gone out of their way for him. But he also had to be honest. Finally he spoke.

"I know I've experienced a lot of stuff . . . but that's all it is—experience. I have nothing to verify that it's true—no scientific proof that any of this really happened. For all I know, this could all be some sort of dream."

Denise let out a sigh of frustration and looked to the Weaver.

The old man was nodding in quiet understanding. Soon his eyes turned to Denise. "And you?" he asked. "You still do not believe in Imager's compassion?"

For a moment the question caught Denise off-guard. Then she remembered that was the other reason they'd come. She knew her answer was no better than Josh's, so she said nothing. Instead she stared at the ground hoping the question would somehow go away.

But the Weaver continued to wait.

Finally she spoke. "How can I?" she asked quietly. "How can I believe in his love, when . . ." She swallowed hard. "When all he does when you try to get close to him is destroy you." Try as she might she couldn't keep from looking back up to the Weaver.

The old man nodded. There was no missing the moisture in his eyes. "Then come," he said softly, "we must not be late." With that he turned and resumed shuffling toward the door.

Denise and Josh glanced at each other and followed. It looked like their adventure wasn't quite over.

Chapter Six

The Machine

"Clickclick   CLICKclickCLICK." Bud continued to test the microphone. He blew into it and stepped a little closer. "Click   CLICK." Suddenly the speakers squealed with feedback. The guests surrounding the outdoor stage cringed in pain. After several agonizing seconds the noise finally stopped, and the folks immediately resumed their smiles and chit-chat. After all, that was Bud up there on stage. Such things should be expected.

Word had come that the Upside-Downers had just left Fayrah and were heading for Biiq. They'd had a couple of minor detours but now they were definitely on their way. Any second Bud would have the honor of welcoming them. Denise's Machine had been tested and re-tested for the thousandth time. It was working perfectly. And across the river, on the other side of Biiq, Olga, the

Kingdom's computer, was humming with life, waiting for Josh.

Everything was set. Now all Bud had to do was greet them and escort them safely to their destinations. A simple task, even for Bud. Well, at least that's what everybody hoped.

"Pssst . . . Pssssssst."

Bud turned around and just happened to see the most beautiful creature he had ever seen in his entire life. Symmetrically she was perfect. Every part of her was the perfect mathematical ratio of another—from the length of her arms to the diameter of her knee caps to the width of her toenails. Don't get me wrong. This lady was not pretty. Not by our standards. But to a scientist and mathematician, she was more breathtaking than an Einstein equation.

"Most important and excellent of all scientists," she spoke with a voice that vibrated in perfect mathematical frequencies. "Please, if you would be so kind as to tell me where I might find the Machine—the one you've prepared for the female Upside-Downer? I have a gift for her."

"Cl-cl-cl-click   cl-click CLICK   cl-click." Even in the language of Biiq you could tell that old Buddy boy was stuttering. The woman's beauty was definitely fogging up his thinking a little.

She frowned slightly, not understanding the clicks.

Realizing she wasn't from Biiq, Bud nervously fumbled for the Translator attached to his belt. He turned it on and repeated himself. It translated his clicks perfectly. Well, almost perfectly. There seemed to be a slight short in the circuit, which made it occasionally repeat a word or two. Then there was the problem of Bud's stuttering. "I'm s-s-sorry s-s-sorry, but that's a s-s-secret s-s-secret," he said. "We have word that s-s-someone is trying to hurt hurt her. S-some s-s-sort of ugly queen queen."

"But what of my gift?" the beautiful lady asked, managing to smile, flirt, and sulk all at the same time.

Bud was hooked. Yessir, she was a pro. Every tone had been carefully measured to capture Bud's heart. And now that she had that, it was just a matter of manipulating it to get her way.

"Surely the most important scientist in the Kingdom could figure out something . . . hmmmm?" She batted her perfectly proportioned eyelids, each with the perfect number of eyelashes.

"D-d-don't worry worry," Bud volunteered, suddenly sounding very gallant. "I'll s-s-ee to it that she gets it it p-p-personally."

"Oh thank you, sir," the lady smiled sweetly as she reached out to touch his arm. "You're as kind a man as you are important."

That cinched it. Bud was in love. No doubt about it. He gave a polite little bow as he took the gift. Then excusing himself (after all he was an important scientist who had important science-type things to do) he turned back toward the microphone. It was then he spotted it— a tiny hole in the corner of the wrapped box. He turned back to the lady but she was already gone.

That's odd, he thought. *Where could she be? Oh well*, he mused, as he waved off a pesky fly that buzzed past, *she's sure to be in the audience admiring my importance. I'll see her then. Maybe even give her a little smile to make her day.* With a confident grin, Bud turned and headed back toward the microphone—not, of course, without the usual trips and stumbles along the way.

Now, if Bud had been a little less in love and a little

more observant, he'd have seen that the lady hadn't disappeared at all. She had only changed. As soon as he had accepted the gift and turned his back, she had reduced herself to a *fly*—a fly with the same black, leathery wings that Denise had seen high over the forest of Keygarp—the same wings she had seen in her dreams. Wings that could only belong to the Illusionist.

The sinister creature buzzed past Bud and squeezed into the little hole that she had cut out of the corner of the gift box. Here she would stay, completely unnoticed. Here, she would hide until she was at the Machine, all alone with Denise.

BEEP . . .
BOP . . .
BURP . . .
BLEEP . . .

Suddenly Listro Q, Aristophenix, Josh, and Denise made their grand and long-awaited entrance into Biiq. It would have been a bit more grand had Listro Q not missed his coordinates again. Instead of landing on the stage, they landed in a nearby tree. Even that wouldn't have been so bad if they had landed *right-side up*. But there they were, all four of them, hanging upside-down in a tree, trying their best to look like proper, distinguished visitors.

"Nice work," Aristophenix muttered between clenched teeth, as he pretended to smile for the crowd.

"Cool," Listro Q answered, as he pretended to be cool.

Denise, on the other hand, was in no mood to pretend anything. "Listro Q!" she shouted. "*LISTRO Q!!*"

But before Listro Q had a chance to defend himself, Bud had begun his speech. "sgniteerG sgniteerg, tsom devoleb edispU-srenwoD srenwoD." He glanced up from

the paper in his hands and smiled. But no one was smiling back. In fact, everyone looked pretty confused, as if they didn't understand a word he was saying. What was going on? What was wrong?

Finally he glanced down at the Translator attached to his belt. Of course! It was shorting out again. Only worse. Now it wasn't just repeating itself, it was also translating backwards! "diputS diputs, doog rof gnihton, on dnarb eman rotalsnarT," he grumbled before giving it a good thwack with his hand. That did the trick. The backwards problem immediately cleared up. Bud grinned, pleased that all his years in electronics school had finally paid off.

He started again. "Greetings greetings, most beloved Upside-Downers Downers. It is with great pleasure pleasure that we welcome you to to the Kingdom of Biiq Biiq—the Kingdom of Math Math and Science."

The audience clapped and clicked enthusiastically—in perfect mathematical unison, of course.

Now, we could go on and on about the ceremony—how everyone was so honored with Denise and Josh's presence, how they gave them the computer code-word to the city, and all that sort of stuff. But the fact is, it bored Denny and Josh to tears (and they were there), so you can imagine how boring it would be to read about it. Let's just say it was a very nice little ceremony and leave it at that, shall we? Good.

Three hours, twenty-four minutes, and eight seconds later (they like to be precise in Biiq), Bud unlocked the massive door to a huge warehouse, revealing the biggest laboratory Denise and Josh had ever seen.

"Wow!" they exclaimed.

Besides the obligatory bubbling beakers and smoking test tubes, there were hundreds of electronic thing-

a-ma-jigs and do-hickeys that glowed and flashed everywhere. Some towered for stories over their heads, others
stretched for hundreds of yards. But no matter how tall
or how long, and no matter how many different colored
lights flashed on how many different panels, they all
seemed to focus on one thing. It was just ahead of them
and not much bigger than a round dinner table. But it
was not a table. It was a thin layer of packed sand that
floated a few feet above the floor. Instead of legs, it was
supported by some sort of powerful energy field that
hummed and buzzed around its circumference.

And one other thing—it glowed. Almost as brightly
as The Center. But it wasn't the sand that was glowing,
it was a thick liquid that spread out across the sandy
surface.

"What . . . what is it?" Denise asked as she slowly
approached.

"The Experiment Experiment," Bud beamed. He was
grinning from ear to ear, unable to hold back his pride.

"For what?"

"For you you."

Denise turned to him in surprise. "What?"

"The only way to clearly clearly understand Imager's
compassion is to clearly clearly understand his heart."

"Yeah, so?"

"So, with this Machine, you will will become a creator. You will gain gain a creator's heart."

Denise just looked at him as if he'd lost his mind.

Aristophenix grinned at her and tried to explain:

What better way
Imager's love to understand,
than to create your own life
and hold it in your hand.

Denise still wasn't catching on. "What are you guys talking about?"

"Denny?" It was Josh. "I think I understand. These guys have set it all up so you can create a life-form." He turned to Bud, "Is that right?"

"Correct correct," Bud agreed.

"And by doing this, they hope you'll experience the same feelings and stuff that this Imager has toward *his* creation."

"Correct again again."

"You're not serious?" Denise asked.

"Oh, yes yes, very serious."

"But . . . but I don't know beans about science. I can't . . . I can't . . . create *life*."

"Don't feel too too bad," Bud chuckled. "Nobody else has had much much luck in that department, either."

"Then how—"

"Imager. His Breath has already been programmed into the Machine."

"What machine?"

"Why, this whole whole laboratory. We've spent the last three and a half epochs building it for you."

Denise just stood there more amazed than ever. "For me? You built all this for *me*?"

Bud nodded. "At Imager's orders."

"But . . . how do I . . . I mean . . . where . . ."

"Don't worry," Bud laughed. "Your only concern concern is this Platform in front of you . . . and this microphone above your head."

"But . . . I still don't . . ."

"All you have to do is speak speak into the microphone. No matter what you say, great or small small, the Machine will translate your words into action. The Machine will make your every word happen happen."

"This is crazy!" Denise protested.

"No," Listro Q answered quietly from behind her. "Imager's love, this is."

She turned to him. "You knew this was planned?"

Listro Q nodded with a gentle smile. "From our meeting, very first."

"If you need any help help," Bud said as he turned to leave, "just tell the Machine and we'll come right right back."

"Wait a minute!" Denise cried in sudden panic. "You're not leaving me!"

"Yes yes. It's important that you do this on your own own. No one must interfere with what you do do. And more importantly, no one must interfere with what you feel feel."

"But I'm sticking around, right?" Josh asked.

"Sorry," Bud answered.

"But *I'm* the one interested in science. I'm the one whose mind needs a rational explana—"

"This isn't about the the mind, Joshua. This is about the the heart."

"Yeah, but—"

"Your studies of logic logic are with with Olga."

"Who?"

"Our computer—the best best in the Kingdom."

Josh scowled slightly, not sure if a question and answer session with some computer rated with getting to create his very own life-form.

Noticing his disappointment, Listro Q spoke. "Worry not to. For you, best Olga will be. Me trust."

Josh gave him a hard look but Listro Q held his gaze.

Bud turned back to Denise. "Call us us whenever you want to quit quit. Anytime, day or night night."

"Day or night! It's going to last that long?"

Bud smiled. "That's up to you you."

Denise looked at the floating Platform with the liquid light spread out across its surface. This was crazy, all of it!

But if it really *was* safe, and if she really *could* quit anytime she wanted to . . . On the other hand, all she had was their word.

She turned to Aristophenix who was smiling, as if reading her thoughts.

Don't be a worryin',
there's nothin' to fear.
To his feelings this will only
help you draw near.

He gave another smile and the slightest of nods—as if to say everything would be OK.

Finally Denny turned to Josh. He was still a shade green with envy as he looked about the huge laboratory or *Machine* as Bud had called it. He was obviously trying his best to be grown up about the whole thing, but he wasn't succeeding too well.

"Well, kiddo . . ." With a little effort he broke into that famous grin of his. "I'd say you're about the luckiest person I've ever met."

Denise tried to smile back. She wanted to tell him how terrified she was by the whole idea, especially the part about being left alone. But the excitement in his eyes suddenly made her feel very stupid—like some little kid afraid of the dark.

"No one's ever had a chance like this," he said, continuing to smile, continuing to be the good sport. "And I doubt anyone ever will."

His words were meant to encourage Denny but they didn't. Instead, they only made her feel more stupid.

Like all this was something she should be grateful for. Something she should feel honored about. Well, maybe she should. After all, Josh was right, no one *had* ever had a chance like this. And it was true, no one probably ever *would*. So how could she refuse? And if she did, how could she ever live with herself afterwards?

It wasn't easy but at last she had her answer. Not so much because it was what she wanted, but because it was what she knew she *should* want. She turned back to Bud and in her best I-can-handle-anything tone said, "When do I start?" She would have been more convincing if her voice didn't quiver toward the end.

"Right away!" Bud grinned.

"Atta girl!" Aristophenix said, slapping her on the back. "It's gonna be great!"

"Oh, here here, I'd almost forgotten." Bud reached out and handed Denny the gift he had been carrying under his arm. "It came from a most extraordinary lady lady who wanted to make sure you got it it."

Denise took the present without paying much attention to it. At the moment she had a few other things on her mind.

After more good lucks, hugs, and see ya soons, the group turned and started for the door.

"Joshua!" Denise suddenly cried out in panic.

"What's up?" he asked, coming to a stop.

But she swallowed hard and shook her head. She'd have to be strong. Even if it killed her, she wouldn't admit her fear—especially to Josh.

The boy flashed her his reassuring grin. "I'd give anything to be in your shoes, kiddo."

Denise smiled back, desperately wishing he were.

Finally he turned and joined the others at the door. Everyone waved and shouted a few more encouraging words. Again Bud reminded her that she could quit any-time she wanted to, and that they'd all see her soon.

Denise waved back.

Bud grasped the huge door and began to slide it shut—until it crunched heavily into his foot. "Oooh, Ouch Ouch!" he cried, grabbing his foot and doing a little jig. "I hate it it when that happens! Ouch, Ooo Ooo, ouch!"

Denise smiled in spite of herself.

After a couple more hops and a few more ouches, Bud gave another wave and finally shut the door. It gave a foreboding *BOOM* that echoed back and forth inside the Machine.

Denise stood there a long moment. Slowly she turned to face the floating Platform. The only thing greater than her excitement was her fear. But Denny had never ad-mitted to being afraid of anything and she wasn't about to start now. So, with a deep breath, she moved toward the Platform of liquid light. She was all alone.

Well, *almost* all alone.

— CHAPTER SEVEN —

THE EXPERIMENT BEGINS

Nearly twelve hours had passed before the Illusionist woke up, stretched her six hairy legs, and quietly crept out of the hole in the corner of the gift box. True, the nap might have been a bit longer than necessary, but even the most evil and hideous creature in seven dimensions needed her beauty rest. Besides, she figured destroying Denise would be a snap. Since they were alone together inside the Machine, it would be a piece of cake (which, now that she was in the form of a fly, sounded pretty appealing, especially the frosting part).

Don't get me wrong. It wasn't that the Illusionist hated Denise. It was just that Imager loved her. And since the Illusionist hated Imager, and since the best way to hurt someone you hate is to destroy someone they love . . . well, you can see why the Illusionist really didn't have much choice in the matter. She *had* to destroy Denise.

But instead of going immediately for the kill, the Illusionist decided to stay disguised as a fly just a little bit longer. That way she could buzz the Machine a few times and check it out—find out what was happening. Even in her part of the Universe, the Illusionist had heard plenty about this new-fangled invention that was being built, and how Imager hoped to instruct an Upside-Downer through it.

Once she was airborne and looking down on Denise and the glowing Platform, the Illusionist suddenly grew sick to her stomach. She was not prepared to see such innocence and goodness, such sweetness and kindness. It was absolutely disgusting, thoroughly nauseating.

With the help of the Machine, Denise had already created two little life-forms in the liquid light. Gus and Gertrude, she called them. Already, the three of them were having the time of their lives, playing, laughing, and joking with one another.

Denny had made them exactly like herself—well, except for the extra set of arms. She'd always thought we human-types were a little short in that department, and she wanted to make sure her creations had every advantage. "This way you can brush your teeth and comb your hair at the same time," she had explained.

Of course it was impossible for her to see the two little folks, because they were so tiny. But she could tell where they were by the ripples they made as they swam and splashed in the liquid light. They couldn't see Denise either. She was too big. In fact, she was so big they figured she was everywhere. In a sense, they were right.

But even though they couldn't see one another, they could hear one another's voices. That was one of the first orders Denise had given to the Machine. And it was one of her best. Now the three of them could talk and joke and laugh for as long as they wanted.

Gus was the funniest. He was all huffy and puffy and pretended to have all the answers, when most of the time he didn't have a clue. How could he? He was only a few hours old! But that didn't stop him from faking it.

Gertie, on the other hand (she made it clear from the start that she hated the name Gertrude), was also a crack-up. The little gal could get so excited over the simplest things . . . "Look, Gus! I have a toe, I have a toe! Look at my toe!" And when she wasn't getting excited about having toes or fingers or a belly button, she was constantly bombarding Denise with a thousand "whys, what ifs, and how comes."

They were incurably cute, reminding Denise of a couple of puppies the way they romped and climbed and played together. Better yet, they reminded her of babysitting the Jefferson twins (when they were on their *best* behavior and when they *didn't* need their diapers changed).

But it was more than just their cuteness and playfulness. There was something else. Denny couldn't put her finger on it, but she'd never felt anything quite like it. As she continued to watch them, her chest began to ache. But it wasn't a bad ache, it was a pleasing ache— a wonderful ache. And the more she hovered over her creations, encouraging them in this new adventure of theirs called *life*, the more wonderful the ache grew. Although she couldn't describe the feeling, it was safe to say that Denny was definitely becoming attached to these little critters.

And they were becoming attached to her. In fact, Gertie put it best when Denny had left them briefly to check out the rest of the Machine. She was gone only a few minutes, but when she returned Gertie stood with her arms folded (all four of them) and began to scold Denise for being gone so long. "It was awful," she complained in her cute little high-pitched voice, "like a part of me was missing. Don't you ever *ever* leave us again!"

"OK, OK," Denise chuckled. "I promise I won't ever *ever* do that again." But even as she joked with her, Denny knew Gertie was right. She *was* a part of them. And they were a part of *her*. And why not? After all, hadn't they come from Denise's own personality and imagination? Gus with his know-it-all and I'll-tackle-the-world mentality, and cute little Gertie with all of her questions and that big, sensitive heart of hers? It was true. Both were definitely a part of Denise, and she was definitely a part of them.

Then it happened.

"Hey, guys!" Gus shouted. "Watch this!"

He was busy showing off to the girls by swimming little figure eights within the liquid light. As he swam faster and faster, the figure eights grew bigger and bigger. Gertie was so impressed that she floated up to the surface to get a better view. But as Gus kept making bigger and bigger waves, she kept getting bobbed up and down, higher and lower.

"WHOA, WOW, WEE . . . OK, Gus," she gasped between bobs, "cut it OUUUUU, WOW, WOOOOO . . . I'm not kidding now, STOHH, EEEEE, OOOOO."

Soon both Denny and Gertie were laughing so hard tears streamed down their cheeks. But not Gus. He was really getting into it. And as his figure eights grew larger and larger he began swimming closer and closer to the Platform's edge.

"OK, Gus," Denise finally called out through her

laughter. "That's enough now."

But Gus didn't hear her.

"OK, Gus," Denise called a little louder.

By now he was much closer to the edge . . . too close. And he still wasn't paying attention.

"Gus . . . Gus!"

No answer.

Denise fought back her rising panic. Any second he could swim out too far; any second he could accidentally swim over the edge and fall to his death.

"GUS!" she shouted.

Sensing her alarm, Gertie also began to call. She wasn't sure why, but the tone in Denny's voice surely meant something was wrong. "Gus!" she cried. "Hey, Gus!"

Still no response.

Denise's panic turned to fear as Gus started the next figure eight—his biggest one yet—the one that would take him straight over the edge. What could she do? How could she stop him?

"GUS . . . GUS, LISTEN TO ME . . . GUS!!"

But Gus didn't hear a word.

Suddenly a thought came to Denny. As a last-ditch effort she quickly turned to the microphone and shouted, "WALL!" There was a slight hum to the Machine. Immediately a wall sprung up near the edge of the Platform. And just in time! It had barely formed before Gus hit it—head on. It was close but Denise had managed to save Gus just before he'd have fallen over the edge to his death.

But instead of showing his appreciation, Gus glared up at the sky. "Hey! What do you think you're doing?" he shouted, rubbing his head.

"You were swimming toward the edge," Denise explained. "I had to stop you with this Wall."

"What do you mean *edge*, what's an edge?"

"It's an, uh, ending . . . that is . . . a . . ." But try as she might, Denise couldn't come up with a word he'd understand. "It's something that would kill you," she finally said.

"What do you mean, *kill*?"

"I mean you would . . . you would stop living and thinking . . . you'd stop . . . existing."

"Go on!" Gus shouted.

"No, I'm serious. Honest."

Gus was still a little steamed. "So why in tarnation didn't you tell me? No offense, but this 'Wall' thing of yours packs a mighty wallop."

"She tried to tell you," Gertie joined in. "She shouted at you over and over again."

"I didn't hear a thing. Just a roar."

"A *roar*?" Denise asked.

"Yeah, a roar that kept getting louder and louder."

Denise glanced at the edge of the Platform. "Oh that . . . that must be the energy field that's holding you up. It's all around the Platform. I guess it just drowned me out."

"What do you mean, *energy field*?" Gus asked.

"Yeah, and what's a *Platform*?" Gertie wondered. "And what do you mean by *drowned*? And what's a—"

"Never mind," Denise laughed, "never mind." If she wasn't careful the two would play their definition game forever. "Let's just say it's a good idea not to get so close to the edge next time."

"You ain't just a-whistlin' *Dixie*," Gus agreed. "That Wall ain't no *treat*, and this *kill* stuff don't sound so hot either. Thanks for the warning."

"No problem." Denise smiled.

But she wouldn't have been smiling if she had known what the Illusionist was thinking. By circling high overhead she had seen everything. Everything from the sickening love and affection between Denise and the creatures to Gus's near-destruction by swimming off the edge.

And as she watched, a plan began to form in her mind. It was one thing to simply destroy Denise, but it was quite another to make her writhe and suffer in agony first. The Illusionist broke into a grin. Writhing and suffering were two of her favorite words.

Soon Denise would be experiencing them both.

Without a moment's hesitation, the Illusionist folded her wings back and dove straight for the Platform. Then just before she splashed into the liquid light, she transformed herself into the shape of Gus and Gertie—complete with four arms.

———

Across the river, on the other side of Biiq, Josh stood in front of another machine—Olga. She was no taller than a man and no thicker than your average run-of-the-mill breakfast waffle, complete, of course, with all those little square holes. Olga snaked in and around the entire Kingdom as far as the eye could see.

"What is it?" Josh asked.

"She's one of the most powerful computers in our our dimension." Bud grinned. "We explore Imager through her. She helps us understand him better better."

Josh took a deep breath. He hated being a pain. At school he was everybody's friend. He worked hard at that. Maybe too hard. But right now he'd had just about all the talk of Imager that he could stand for one day.

"Look," he began politely. "I appreciate what you're

trying to do. But there's no way you can prove to me that there's some sort of . . . supreme being out there, someone who knows all and sees all. At least not through science."

Bud started to speak, but Josh wasn't finished. "I'm not saying there isn't something. I mean I definitely saw and experienced some stuff at The Center. But it's like I told the Weaver . . . to try to prove it scientifically . . . well, forget it—it's just not possible."

Bud smiled at Aristophenix and Listro Q, then reached over and pressed a single button on the computer. Immediately a paper-thin sheet of water shot out of Olga and floated before them. It was only three feet long and a foot wide, but it was enough to make Josh jump back in surprise.

"Don't worry worry. It's only a projected image," Bud said. "See?" He ran his hands through the picture. "Just like at the movies."

Josh reached out and touched the water. It was true. There really was no water, just a picture floating in mid-air.

"Tell me me," Bud asked. "What do you know know about geometry?"

"A little. We haven't had it at school yet or anything, but I've done some reading."

"Good good. In the Upside-down Kingdom, how many dimensions do you live in in?"

"Well . . . three. We have three dimensions. Everything in our world has some length to it, that's one dimension; some width, that's two dimensions; and some height, that's three dimensions. Everything from a pea to a skyscraper has three dimensions."

"Very good. But what if there were more more than three dimensions?"

"Some scientists say time is a fourth dimension."

Bud couldn't help smiling. "Interesting theory. But could five, six, seventy or seven hundred dimensions also exist? Is that that possible?"

"Mathematically, sure. But we could never see them. They'd be past our understanding."

"Precisely."

"Hold it, wait a minute. Are you saying this Imager guy is in a dimension higher than ours?"

"The highest."

"But . . . if that's true . . . well, you could never prove him."

"Yes and no," Bud answered. "The only way way to understand a higher dimension is to use use the dimensions we already have."

Josh looked at him, waiting for more.

"Say this rectangle floating in front front of us were only two dimensions. It has length," he ran his hand along the three-foot side of the floating picture, "and it has width." He reached across the shorter, one-foot end. "But it has no height, no tallness. In other words words, there's a back and forth and a sideways, but no up and down."

Josh nodded. *So far, so good.*

"Now, let's say say there are people living in this two-dimensional world—a world completely flat flat. They would have no understanding of up and down, correct?"

Josh nodded again.

"How would would we in the third dimension look to those two-dimensional people?"

"If they looked up, we'd look like giants staring down at them."

"No no . . . they wouldn't know how to look up. Remember, they have no up or down. All they have in their two-dimensional world is back and forth and a side-ways."

"Well then, I guess . . . they'd never be able to see us at all."

"Precisely precisely. Does that mean we wouldn't be here?"

"No, we'd be here. And we could see everything about them, all the time, from one end of this rectangle to the other. We could see their whole life."

"And if we wanted them to see see us what would we do do?"

"I guess we'd have to get down to their level." Josh began to chuckle. "It sure would be a shock to them, though." He reached toward the floating picture. "It would be like, *poof*—" He stuck the tip of his finger into the picture. "We'd suddenly appear, then *poof*—" He pulled his finger out. "We'd suddenly disappear."

"But would we really disappear?"

"No . . . like I said, we'd be here with them all along. But to them, we'd be like these . . . these . . ." Josh came to sudden stop. The thought boggled his mind for a moment. He looked up to Bud, his eyes widening with understanding.

"What would we be like to them, Josh Josh?" Bud gently asked. He already knew the boy had the answer.

After a moment, Josh slowly spoke the words. "To them we'd be like . . . we'd be all-knowing, all-seeing." Josh swallowed hard. Then after another pause he continued. "To them we'd be like . . . like . . . God."

— CHAPTER EIGHT —

CHOICES

A lot had happened during the time Denise had dozed off. Dozing off was the last thing she had in mind, particularly after Gertie's lecture about not leaving them. But after a day of school, traveling, visiting The Center, nearly seeing Imager, ceasing to exist, being rewoven, and all the hours of joy and excitement with Gus and Gertie, well, she didn't have much choice. She was just going to lie down for a second to rest her eyes. Unfortunately, that second turned into almost an hour. And an Illusionist can do a lot of damage in almost an hour.

The first thing Denise noticed when she rose to her feet and looked toward the Platform was that the Wall she'd created had a hole in it. The second thing she noticed was that on the other side of the Wall, just a hairsbreadth from the edge, were Gus's ripples. He was shouting and having a good old time.

"GUS!! GUS WHAT ARE YOU DOING?" she cried as she raced to the Platform. "GET AWAY FROM THE EDGE! GUS . . . GUS!!"

But Gus couldn't hear her. He was too close to the edge. The roar was too loud.

A wave of desperation washed over Denise. Any second he would lose his balance. Any second he would fall onto the floor and be destroyed! What could be done?

Then she remembered . . . the Machine!

She spun around to the microphone and yelled, "Machine! Pick up Gus and put him back into the center of—"

"Not so fast, dear heart."

The voice sent a chill through Denny. She recognized it at once. She had heard it a thousand times in her dreams, and high over the trees of Keygarp. But now . . . now it was coming from somewhere on the Platform!

"What are you doing here?" Denise shouted, trying to push back the fear, as she desperately searched for a telltale ripple in the liquid light. "Where are you?"

"I'm right over here."

"Where?" Denise demanded.

"Why, with Gertie, of course."

Denise gasped. *The Illusionist—with Gertie?*

"Hi, Denny," Gertie's voice called out as cheerfully as ever.

"Hi Gertie," Denise answered slowly and cautiously as her eyes continued to search the Platform. Finally she spotted them. Two ripples near the center. She continued to talk, trying to keep her voice calm and steady. Whatever was happening, she didn't want to scare her sensitive little friend. "What . . . what's going on, Gertie? What's Gus doing?"

"Oh, he's just exercising his *free will*."

"His what?"

"The Lady here explained it all to us," Gertie chirped. "If Gus wants to play at the edge he has every right to."

"That's right," the Illusionist encouraged. Her voice was smooth and seductive. "Otherwise you'd be living in a prison, wouldn't you?"

"Uh-huh," Gertie agreed, "and Denny wouldn't want that."

"No, of course she wouldn't," the Illusionist cooed. "Because Denny loves you, doesn't she?"

"With her whole heart," Gertie added.

Suddenly the air was split with a piercing scream. "AHHHHHHH . . ."

Denise whirled to the edge of the Platform. The little ripples that had surrounded Gus were gone. Instead, there was just a pinpoint glimmer of a reflection falling from the Platform.

It was Gus!

Without thinking, Denise dove headfirst toward the reflection, flying through the air, arms outstretched, hands open. It was close, but somehow, some way, just before she hit the floor, she felt the faintest tickle inside her palm. Gus had landed safely in her open hand.

"WOOOO-EEEEEE!" he shouted as Denise rolled onto her back and struggled to her feet. "That was somethin'! Hey, Gertie, if you can hear me, you ought to come over and try this!"

"What do you mean?" Denise shouted angrily at him. "You could have killed yourself. Gus . . . GUS!"

"It will do no good, dear heart," the Illusionist chuckled. "He can't hear you. You know that—not near the edge."

"Fine, then I'll put him back in the middle where he . . ."

"But he doesn't want to be in the middle. He wants to be at the edge."

"I know that, but—"

"She's got a point, Denny." It was Gertie again—just as sweet and thoughtful as ever. "You wouldn't want to make him live someplace he didn't want to. You want him to exercise his free will, right?"

There was that phrase again. Already Denise was beginning to hate it. For a moment she was tempted to shout, *I don't care about your stupid free will! I'm the boss and what I say goes!* But she didn't. Somehow she knew that being a demanding bully wasn't exactly what their friendship was about. So she tried to reason.

"Look, I know that's what he wants—to play on the edge. But I also know it will kill him. So I have to tell him."

"But you already did," the Illusionist gently reminded her. "And he chose not to listen."

"But he listened to you, didn't he?" There was no missing the anger growing in Denny's voice.

"I have my ways," the Illusionist chuckled.

"Yeah, well I have mine, too." With a determined voice Denise turned and spoke into the microphone. "Machine, I want you to take this, this stranger here, and I want you to—"

"Hold on, missy."

Denise stopped.

"So what are you going to do—destroy me?"

"The thought had crossed my mind."

"That's rich," the Illusionist laughed easily. "So is that what you do? Destroy anyone who disagrees with you?"

"No, of course she wouldn't." Gertie's little voice was

also sounding a little angry now. "Denny isn't that way. Are you Denny?"

"Well, no . . ." Denise faltered, "of course not."

"See?" Gertie challenged, "Denny loves us."

"Love," the Illusionist sneered. "You call this love? Making people live where they don't want to live . . . destroying those that don't agree with her? That is not love."

Once again the tops of Denise's ears were starting to burn. She'd had enough talk. Now it was time for action. "Machine," she shouted, "I want you to take this, this thing and—"

"I guarantee you!" the Illusionist shouted over her.

In spite of herself, Denise stopped to listen.

"If you destroy me, I guarantee that Gus and Gertie will never love you on their own. They'll only pretend to love you. They'll be afraid that if they don't, you'll destroy them just as you did me!"

Denise's head was swimming. She knew there was some truth to the Illusionist's words. She also knew that she wanted to wipe the creature off the face of the Platform. And if those weren't enough feelings flying around, there was also her intense worry over Gus.

"Why . . ." She turned back to the Illusionist. The emotion was rising to her throat now. "Why are you doing this to us? Things were so good before. Everything was so perfect."

"Since when is a dictatorship perfect?" the Illusionist demanded.

"But I'm no dictator, I'm . . . I'm—"

"Hey, are you going to put me down or what!" Gus demanded.

Denise looked in her palm.

"Put me on the edge; put me on the edge!" he shouted.

"I want to jump off again, I want to jump off again!"

Denise stared down into her hand, angry at the tears that were welling up in her eyes. "Gus," she stammered, "don't you see. It will kill you."

But he didn't hear. He didn't answer.

"Gus . . . please . . ." By now the tears were forming faster than Denny could blink them away. "Please . . . listen to me . . . Gus . . ."

"Cry all you want," the Illusionist taunted, "but he'll never hear you. It was his choice. He'll never hear you again!"

The words pierced deep into Denny's heart. One of her closest and best friends was trying to kill himself. No, he was more than a best friend. He was a part of her. A part of her was trying to kill himself, and there was nothing she could do to stop him.

"Gus . . ." she croaked hoarsely, "please . . ."

But there was no answer—except the continual demands of, "Put me down," and "I want to jump off the edge."

"Isn't there . . ." She looked back to the Platform where the Illusionist was, hoping for some way, *any* way out. "Isn't there *something* I can do?"

"Not a thing," the Illusionist cooed.

Denny looked back to her palm. She stood there a long moment listening to Gus's insistent shouts.

The Illusionist was right. Denise could demand that Gus stay in the middle, but then she'd be a dictator. She could build an impregnable wall around him, but then she'd be a prison guard. She could wipe out the Illusionist, but then she'd be a murderer.

The realization pressed heavily on her chest, making it hard to breathe. The knot in her throat continued to tighten. But there was nothing she could do. She could see that now. She had no alternative.

"Gus . . . please?"

"Put me down! Put me down! Put me down!" was his only reply.

Denny listened a few moments longer—her mind racing and probing every possibility. But there was no way out.

"Gus," she pleaded one last time.

His answer was the same.

Then, ever so slowly, Denise lowered her hand back toward the edge of the Platform. "Goodbye, dear friend," she whispered softly.

"Put me down! Put me down!"

"Goodbye . . ."

She saw the ripples as he jumped out of her hand and back into the liquid light.

"Don't worry, Denny." It was Gertie. She was also crying. "You still have me. And I'll never leave you. I promise I'll never, never leave you."

Denise tried to smile. Good old Gertie. Always the sensitive, big-hearted Gertie. But wait! Suddenly a thought came to her mind. Of course, why hadn't she thought of it before? It was a long shot. But maybe . . .

"EEEEE—HHHHAAAA . . ." It was Gus once again, racing toward the edge of the Platform and leaping off.

Immediately Denise slid her hand underneath the edge and caught him.

"What are you doing?" the Illusionist yelled. "You're depriving him of his free will!"

But Denise paid no attention. "Gertie!" she called. "Gertie, will you do me a favor?"

"Of course, Denny, whatever you want."

"Will you give a message to Gus?"

"Now wait a minute," the Illusionist protested, "that's not fair."

"Of course it's fair!" Denise grinned, wiping away her tears with a free hand. "He may not be able to hear me, but there's nothing that says I can't write him a note."

"Put me down!" Gus shouted from her palm. "Put me down!"

"Unfair!" the Illusionist insisted, her voice growing higher and shriller. "Unfair!"

Denise was no longer listening. "Machine," she commanded, "write a message. Put it on something that will last and see to it that Gertie gets it."

The Machine hummed a moment in preparation, and awaited further orders.

"This is unfair!" the Illusionist kept shouting. "Stop it at once!"

"Put me down! Put me down!" Gus kept demanding.

But Denise wasn't stopping for anyone. She'd found the solution. Speaking to the Machine she ordered, "Have the message read: DO NOT JUMP OFF THE EDGE—IT WILL KILL YOU!"

"*Put me down! Put me down!*" Gus squirmed in Denny's hand.

"*Unfair! Unfair!*" the Illusionist cried.

The Machine gave a faint crackle. Suddenly there was another ripple in the liquid light as a large steel sign appeared in front of Gertie.

It was more than the Illusionist could bear. As quickly as the sign appeared, she disappeared. One minute she was there, the next minute she was gone. Neither Gertie nor Denise knew where she went and both hoped they would never see her again.

Unfortunately, their hopes would be short-lived.

CHAPTER NINE

THE SIGN

"Oh, look," Gertie sighed, as she slowly drifted toward the large steel sign. It rested on the floor of her liquid light ocean. "It's so . . . so . . . beautiful."

The truth is, the sign wasn't really that beautiful—just an ordinary sign with a message painted on it. But the fact that it came from her creator, from Denny, brought tears of gratitude to young Gertie's eyes. "Thank you so much," she kept repeating over and over again. "Thank you so very much."

Denise was deeply touched. It seemed the tiniest of things brought joy to Gertie. And somehow that made Denise love her all the more.

"You're so beautiful," Gertie exclaimed, as she tenderly reached out to touch the sign. "And your letters . . . they're so . . . they're printed so perfectly."

For a moment Denise was confused. Who was Gertie

talking to? Then realizing Gertie wasn't addressing her, but the sign, Denise politely cleared her throat. "Ah, Gertie . . . Gertie, it's me, Denny . . . I'm still up here."

"Oh, sorry." Gertie gave an embarrassed giggle as she glanced up to the sky. "I knew that."

Denise smiled. "Now listen, I need you to take that message to—"

"Put me down, put me down!" It was Gus. Denise had almost forgotten he was still in her palm. She lowered her hand and let him jump back onto the edge of the Platform before she quickly returned to Gertie. Unfortunately, Gertie was already in the middle of another conversation—

"Wonderful sign . . . perfect sign . . ."

"Gertie?"

"Your letters speak such truth, such—"

"Gertie . . ."

But Gertie was so busy admiring the sign she barely heard Denise.

"*Gertie!*"

That did the trick. "Oh . . . uh, hi, Denny." But even as she answered, she sounded a little confused, a little distracted. "What were we . . . talking about?"

"Will you ask Gus to look at the sign for me?"

"Of course, I would love to."

"Thank you," Denise said. "I'll order the Machine to move it over to him, and then you can tell him—"

"Oh, no, I can carry it," Gertie volunteered cheerfully.

Denise couldn't help smiling. Once again she was moved by her friend's desire to help. But she didn't need the help. "That's OK," Denise answered, "there's no need for you—"

"No, no, I'd love to carry it for you."

"Thanks Gertie, but I don't think—"

"You're *so* beautiful!" Gertie's voice was sounding foggy again. "Your letters are so perfect; so full of truth. I'll carry you wherever you want to go."

"Gertie, it's just a sign. You're talking to a—"

"I'll carry you anywhere—forever and ever."

"Gertie . . . Gertie!"

But Gerty no longer answered. Before Denise could stop her, she took the huge sign into her four hands and with great effort heaved it onto her back. It was so heavy that she sank deep into the sandy ocean floor. It was so large that it stretched out far over her head. But she forced herself to start walking—the awful weight causing her to groan with every step. Yet Gertie seemed happy to bear the weight. Honored to bear it. She would do anything for her Denny. Anything.

"Gertie!" Denise felt a twinge of panic. "Gertie, listen to me!"

But Gertie could not hear her. The steel plate that stretched out over her head blocked all sound from above.

"Gertie, listen to me!"

Gertie continued to stagger forward, groaning under the weight, completely deaf to Denny's voice. But That's-OK-Gertie didn't need to listen to Denise. Not anymore. After all, she had more important things to do.

"Please, Gertie . . ." Denise could feel the emotion starting to rise in her throat again. Could it be? First she'd lost Gus and now . . . "Gertie! Listen to me!"

But her voice continued to bounce off the steel plate. Suddenly Denny felt very alone. "You're cutting me off," she called. "Gertie, please . . . please don't do this!"

There was no answer.

Gus gave another scream as he jumped off the Platform. Denise leaped forward to catch him. But again, at his insistence, she put him back on the edge—none too gently this time.

"Hey! Watch it!" he shouted before starting his dance toward the edge again.

Denise was confused. Something had to be done. Gertie could never carry that sign—not for long. She wasn't designed to carry it. She'd wear herself out. In desperation Denny turned back to the Machine and gave another order. "Machine . . . another sign."

The Machine hummed in preparation.

"Have it read: LISTEN TO ME!"

The Machine gave a faint crackle and immediately the sign appeared in front of Gertie.

But to Denise's horror Gertie didn't stop to read it. Instead, her gruntings and groanings became twice as loud. Instead of obeying the sign, Gertie had added it to the other one already on her back!

"NO!" Denise shouted.

But she was too late. Now Gertie's burden was doubly hard to carry. Now it was even more impossible for her to hear Denise's warnings.

"Gertie!" she cried. "Please don't do this to yourself! Please, listen to me." Feeling a little lightheaded, Denise grabbed the edge of the Platform for support and watched as Gertie's ripples of light moved slower and slower. The poor little thing was obviously wearing herself out.

Although Denise couldn't see it, the weight of Gertie's load was causing her to sink deeper and deeper into the sandy bottom. That's why the ripples of light were growing so weak. With every step forward Gertie sank deeper. In just a matter of minutes she was waist-deep and sinking fast. Soon the ocean floor would swallow her. The sand would cover her neck, her mouth, her nose; and then, in her stubborn desire to serve Denise, Gertie would suffocate.

"Ahhhh," Gus screamed as he jumped off the edge. Denise dove forward and caught him, then returned to Gertie. But Gertie was gone! There was no more sound, no ripples!

"Gertie!"

Desperately and without thinking Denny shoved her free hand deep into the liquid light where she had last seen Gertie's ripples. It was an impulsive move that could crush her little friend, but she had to do something.

At the same time Gus resumed his demands, "Put me down, put me down!"

Then Denny heard her. She was coughing up sand and screaming hysterically, but there was no mistaking Gertie's high-pitched little voice. "Let me go, let me go!"

For a moment the tiniest wave of relief washed over Denise. But it lasted only a moment.

"Put me down! Put me down!"

"Let me go! Let me go!"

"Stop this!" Denise shouted into both of her hands. "You two are killing yourselves! Don't you see? Stop it!"

But neither was listening.

"PUT ME DOWN! LET ME GO! PUT ME DOWN! LET ME GO" their voices blended into one.

Then another voice joined in. Denise wasn't sure where it came from, but there was no mistaking who it was. "You must let them go, dear heart, or they will be your prisoners. Without free will you become their dictator."

"BUT THEY'LL KILL THEMSELVES!" Denise shouted, her voice echoing throughout the huge room.

"PUT ME DOWN! LET ME GO! PUT ME DOWN . . ."

Moisture was again forming in Denny's eyes. She was completely cut off from both her friends now. Not only that, but they were destroying themselves. Her two best friends were destroying themselves and there was nothing she could do to stop them!

Her throat ached by now and the pressure in her chest was so strong she had to fight to breathe. "Please, Gus," she begged, "Gertie— Please, you two have to listen to me." Her head grew lighter and lighter as she struggled for breath. Hot tears spilled from her eyes and ran down her face.

"YOU NEED ME!" she screamed in anger. "LISTEN TO ME! YOU NEED ME!"

But there was no answer. Only their continual demands—

"PUT ME DOWN! LET ME GO! PUT ME DOWN!"

"Please . . ." Denise's breathing had turned to gasps: Her eyes began to blur. The hours without sleep, the intense emotions, and the ongoing fight to save those she loved was more than she could handle.

Gus and Gertie were now in a mindless rage. Suddenly they added a new phrase to their shouting: "I HATE YOU! I HATE YOU! LET ME GO! PUT ME DOWN! I HATE YOU! I HATE YOU!"

The words smashed into Denise's chest. Her head began to reel. She had only fainted once in her life. She hated the feeling then, and she hated it now. She knew she had to fight it off. But she also knew something else. She knew the Illusionist was right. She knew there was absolutely nothing more she could do.

Slowly, sadly, Denise uncurled her fist. Her mind screamed with anguish as Gus jumped off into the liquid light and back to the edge of the Platform—for the very last time.

And then, no longer able to see through her tears or to stop the room as it started to spin, Denny lowered her other hand. But at the last second she pulled it back. "NO!" she screamed, "I CAN'T!"

"LET ME GO! LET ME GO!" Gertie insisted.

"NO-OOO!"

"LET ME GO! I HATE YOU! LET ME GO!"

"You have no choice, dear heart," the gentle voice purred. "You know that. No choice . . ."

Denise was weeping openly now. But the Illusionist was right, there was nothing she could do. Once again she lowered her hand and slowly opened it. Once again she felt the stab of pain in her heart as Gertie dove into the liquid light and swam toward her precious signs.

Denise tried to say something, anything, but as she clung helplessly to the Platform, no words would come.

Suddenly her tears turned to sobs—gulping, gut-wrenching sobs—Denise wasn't just losing her friends, she was losing her heart. She had never cried like that before, but then she had never felt such pain.

It was cold in the laboratory now—fiercely cold.

Denny could no longer stand and watch. The pressure was too great. Hanging on to the edge of the Platform, she slowly eased herself down to the floor. The sobs continued, only now they were silent sobs—sobs of hopelessness.

She released her grip on the Platform and drew herself into a tiny little ball on the cold concrete floor.

The ache in her chest was unbearable.

— Chapter Ten —

Another Last Chance

Across the river with Bud and the guys, Josh was still learning about Imager. He didn't believe everything they said, but gradually, scientific theory by scientific theory, mathematical formula by mathematical formula, Josh was beginning to realize there must be *somebody* out there.

"But what about the future?" he asked. "Everybody—you guys, the Weaver, all those folks at Fayrah say this Imager knows our future, that he knows what I'm going to do before *I* do."

Aristophenix, Listro Q, and Bud all nodded in agreement.

"But that's impossible!"

"Impossible more it is, that he doesn't," Listro Q offered.

"How?"

Bud grinned. "It's simple. If you would just just imagine—"

"No imaginings," Josh said firmly. "Your theory about higher dimensions is interesting but that's all it is—theory. I need verifiable proof—either through scientific observations or mathematical equations."

Aristophenix and Listro Q exchanged glances. This was going to be tough, or so they thought. Apparently they'd forgotten they were dealing with the great Bud from Biiq.

Without a word Bud pushed four buttons on Olga. Immediately a paper several feet long rolled out of the slot.

"What's that?"

"Your future future."

"Get out of here," Josh scoffed.

But Bud was perfectly serious. "Every one of your personality traits is given given a number. See . . ." He held the paper out, but an immediate frown crossed his face. "This is strange strange. All the information seems to be be printed upside-down."

Josh looked over his shoulder a moment, and then without a word gently took the paper from Bud and turned it right-side up.

"Oh, thank you. Much better better," Bud grinned sheepishly. "Now where where were we?"

"Something about my personality traits having a number?"

"Precisely. Your sports ability is number 706, your friendliness at school school is 245, your desire to please people—"

"Wait a minute, how do you know all that about me?"

"We know everything about you you."

"*Everything?*"

"Everything," Bud grinned. "Remember, we look down down from a higher dimension."

"Oh, yeah, right," Josh swallowed a little uncomfortably. He wasn't so thrilled about all he ever did being watched.

"Anyway," Bud continued. "Everything about you is given a number and everything that could happen to you is given given another number. Then, using the laws of probability we run these numbers numbers through the computer and it tells us exactly what you'll do do in every situation."

"What if I change my mind?"

"You can change your mind mind as often as you want, but we know what your final decision will be be."

"No kidding?"

"And we can predict how that decision will affect other people people in their mathematical future."

"And if you put all of our mathematical futures together . . ."

"We know the entire future future of your world."

"Incredible."

"No," Bud answered. "Just Imager's mathematics."

"Can I see it?" Josh asked, reaching for the paper.

"No, uh, I don't think so so."

"Why not, it's *my* future!"

"According to these figures figures, you would try to alter these numbers."

"No way!" Josh protested.

"Yes, you would."

"Absolutely not."

"Like you didn't try to alter the Weaver's tapestry?"

"Well, that was different."

"How how?"

"Well, because, I mean, that is . . ." Josh was running

out of arguments. As much as he hated to admit it, Bud had a point. "Well, OK, I guess maybe I might try—just a little."

The grouped chuckled quietly. Even Josh had to smile. Then an idea came to mind. "What about Denny?" he asked. "Could I see her future?"

Bud glanced to Aristophenix and Listro Q. They hesitated a moment, then nodded in approval. Bud reached over and pressed four more of Olga's buttons. Immediately another long sheet of paper shot out.

Bud picked it up and began showing the figures to Josh. "See, this number is your friend's stubbornness, this one is her doubts doubts over Imager's love—the reason she came here in the first place."

Josh nodded.

"This is her love for the creatures she's just just created over at the Machine. And this . . . this—" Bud's voice trailed off. Suddenly he grew very pale.

"What is it?" Josh asked.

"No no, this can't be right." Immediately Bud re-pushed the buttons on the computer and immediately another sheet of paper shot out.

"What's wrong?" Josh asked as Bud quickly scanned the paper.

Bud's face grew even whiter.

"Bud?" Aristophenix asked. There was no missing the concern growing in his own voice. "Bud?"

Finally the scientist spoke. "According to these calculations, Denny is experiencing a love for her creation similar to Imager's."

"Well, that's great," Josh exclaimed. "I mean that's what she wanted to understand, right?"

Still staring at the figures, Bud could only shake his head. "Too similar," he quietly murmured, "too similar."

"Similar much how?" Listro Q cautiously ventured. "Similar how, Imager's love to?"

Slowly Bud looked up. "Completely," he said. "A love so similar that it would destroy itself to save its creation."

An icy chill swept over the group.

Then, without a word, Aristophenix quickly turned and started waddling down the path toward the bridge.

"Where are you going?" Josh shouted.

The pudgy creature called from over his shoulder:

Our tooshes should be a movin',
'cause I'm afraid if they don't,
Denny's chances of livin'
are less than remote!

Without a word the others turned and raced after him.

———

Denise wasn't sure when the idea first came. But there, curled up on the cold floor, she realized she hadn't tried everything. There was still one last chance to save her friends.

She struggled to her knees. Then with even more effort, she rose unsteadily to her feet. A wave of dizziness swept over her but she wouldn't give in. Those were her friends on that Platform and nothing would stop her from trying one last time.

She glanced quickly over to the edge. Gus's ripples were still there. Good. That meant he hadn't jumped off yet. Apparently he enjoyed teetering on the edge as much as he did the actual falling.

Next she looked for Gertie's ripples. To her amazement her little friend had already reached the Wall. Gertie's fierce determination surprised her. But then Gertie was part of her, and if there was one thing Denise was full of it was determination. But Gertie's ripples were much fainter than before. As with Gus, it was just a matter of minutes before she'd destroy herself completely.

It was an awful risk. Denise didn't even know if the Machine could pull it off—let alone if she'd survive. Then there was the matter of coming back. But it was the only hope Gus and Gertie had. If they wouldn't let her help them from above, then maybe, just maybe she could help them from beside.

"MACHINE!" she shouted.

Again the Machine hummed in readiness.

"Put me in their world! Make me like Gus and Gertie!"

The Machine crackled and sparked a little longer than usual. After all, this was no easy request. But at last its programs were set and the Machine whirred into action.

Immediately Denise was shrunk to the size of a pinhead and transported into Gus and Gertie's world.

The whole process caught her a little off-guard. Being shrunk to a pinhead is not your everyday experience. Then there was the matter of having to swim and breath in the liquid light. And finally, let's not forget the four arms. It took a lot of concentration not to get them tangled up and even more to keep from accidentally clobbering herself with them. But finally she got the hang of it. And just in time.

"Who are you?"

The voice was faint and weak but Denise recognized it immediately. "Gertie?" she shouted, quickly looking around. "Gertie, where are you?"

"I'm right here," Gertie groaned. "Down here."

Denise looked down to the sandy ocean floor and let out a gasp. By now Gertie had sunk up to her neck. Yet, she still hung on to the heavy signs—holding them high over her head. Nothing would make her let go.

"Quick, let me have those," Denise shouted as she swam toward Gertie and grabbed hold of the signs.

"What are you doing!" Gertie shouted in alarm. "These are Denny's signs, let go of them, let go of them!"

"Gertie, give them to me!"

"Let go, let go!"

There was a little struggle, but being stuck up to her neck in sand tended to hamper Gertie's efforts a bit. Still, her four hands gripped the signs so tightly that it was all Denny could do to pry them loose. Then, despite Gertie's screams of protest, Denise raised the heavy signs high over her head and threw them to the side.

"Noooo!" Gertie screamed. She started to fight and claw her way out of the sand. Denise reached down to help but Gertie would have none of it. At last she dug herself out. But instead of throwing her arms around her creator, as Denise had hoped and dreamed, Gertie raced to the signs and threw her arms around *them*.

"These are Denny's," she cried. "She told *me* to carry them!"

"Gertie, I *am* Denny!"

But Gertie wasn't listening. Instead she comforted and soothed the signs. "Perfect signs, beautiful signs . . ." she said, gently stroking their surfaces. "Did that mean, awful creature scratch you, hmmm?"

Denise approached her cautiously. "Gertie—Gertie, it's me, Denny."

But there was no response as Gertie continued to talk to the signs.

"Gertie, please it's—"

Suddenly Gertie turned on her. "Stay back!" she screamed, pulling the signs in closer for protection.

Denise stopped, puzzled and perplexed. "Gertie?"

"I don't know who you are or what you want, but keep your hands off my signs!"

"Gertie, it's me—Denny."

"LIAR!"

"What?"

"Liar!" Gertie repeated. "Denny would never hurt these signs—Denny would never take them away. These are good signs, perfect signs." She began to rock back and forth, ever so slightly—like a lost child clinging to a doll.

"Of course they're good signs," Denise soothed as she slowly resumed her approach. "That's why I made them. But look what's written on them, look what they—"

"STAY BACK!" Gertie screamed.

Denise slowed, but she didn't stop. "They say you have to quit hurting yourself and pay attention to me."

"Stay back, I said!"

"But you're so busy carrying *them* and loving *them*, that you don't even hear *me*."

"These are perfect signs, good signs," Gertie repeated.

"I know they're good signs, but you're not following them." By now she was nearly at Gertie's side.

"Denny told me to carry them!"

"No, I didn't." Gently, carefully Denise knelt beside her friend. "That was your idea. I just wanted you to obey them. You don't have to carry them."

"But I . . . I . . ." Gertie sounded a little lost—like she really wanted to believe Denise, but like it was too good to be true. "I love Denny . . ." she faltered, "I love Denny and, and she wants me to . . ."

"No," Denise gently answered. "All I want is your safety . . . and to be your friend."

"But I . . . I have to help."

Again Denise shook her head. "By trying to help, you were cutting me off."

By now Gertie was starting to cry. "No . . . that's not true. I . . . I love Denny, I didn't mean to—"

"I know . . ." Denise said, feeling the tears well up in her own eyes. She tenderly wrapped her arms around Gertie. "I know."

Barely aware of it, Gertie returned the hug. So there the two sat for several moments—each giving and needing the other's embrace. Slowly the anger and hurt began to fade. Slowly the love and affection began to return.

Finally Denise reached for the signs. "Here," she gently offered. "Let me help you with those. Let me help you take—"

"NO!" Gertie snarled, pulling back. She was no longer the lost child clinging to her doll. Suddenly she was a starved animal fighting over a scrap of meat. "These are Denny's signs," she growled, "perfect signs, good signs."

"But if you'd just—"

Then with incredible determination, Gertie hoisted the signs over her head and threw them onto her back.

"Gertie, no—"

The poor thing let out an awful groan as the weight crushed her body. But she wouldn't stop. These signs were her life. They had been given to her, and nothing would make her part with them.

"Gertie, please . . ."

There was no answer. Gertie turned and staggered toward the giant hole in the Wall. Every step forced a moan of agony, and every step pushed her deeper and deeper into the sand.

"GERTIE, PLEASE LISTEN TO ME!"

But she would not listen to Denise. She was too devoted to helping her.

CHAPTER ELEVEN

FIGHT OF LOVE

Josh was the first to arrive outside the Machine's giant door. He was followed by Bud, Listro Q, and eventually poor Aristophenix who, as usual, was bringing up the rear and gasping for air.

"Come on!" Josh called over his shoulder. "Hurry!"

At last Aristophenix arrived, wheezing out an apology.

I'm so sorry that I'm tardy,
but we've run so very far,
and we poets are artists
not Olympic track stars.

Josh found himself cringing. No matter how many times he'd heard Aristophenix's awful poetry, he still hadn't quite gotten used to it. He reached for the door and with a mighty heave tried to slide it open.

It wouldn't budge, not an inch.

"Wrong, what's?" Listro Q asked.

"It must be locked," Josh said, trying to push it again, with exactly the same result.

All three looked to Bud. Suddenly he remembered. "Oh, the keys, of course, the keys keys." He reached into his coat pocket as he crossed to the door. "Can't get inside without the keys keys." But there was nothing inside his pocket. So he tried the other. "Yessir, it always helps to have the keys keys." Still nothing. Next he tried his pants pockets. "The keys keys," he muttered, turning to the group. "By the way, have any of you seen them them?"

They all stared at him blankly.

"No, I guess you haven't," he murmured and immediately started through his pockets again.

"Where last use them you did?" Listro Q asked.

"Why, right here at this door door," Bud insisted. "I unlocked this door door and then put the keys keys someplace where I'd be sure to remember."

"Where was that?" Josh asked, already fearing the worst.

Bud looked at him and shrugged. "I don't remember."

The group groaned.

"Wait a minute!" he shouted. "Of course! I put them someplace safe safe where no one could find them."

"Where?" everyone shouted in unison.

"Why, right on the console beside Denny."

The group stared at him in disbelief. Once again he shrugged.

Then, without a word, all four began banging on the door. "Denny! Denny, can you hear us? Denny! Denny open up!"

But Denny couldn't hear. Not a thing.

The group could, though, and what they heard brought a look of surprise to all of their faces. It was an electronic sound and one they all recognized . . .

BEEP . . .
   BOP . . .
      BURP . . .
         BLEEP . . .

"Gertie, please!" Denise shouted. "You've got to listen to me!"

By now Gertie was dragging herself through the hole in the Wall. The bone-crushing weight of the signs took their toll with every step, but she had to get away. Denny had started to make sense and that was something Gertie could not stand.

But Denise wouldn't be shaken. She stayed right at her side. "Gertie, please," she reasoned, "let me carry those . . . please."

At last they passed through the hole and looked ahead. For a moment neither could say a word.

"Hey, Gertie, who's your friend?" It was Gus. He was standing right on the edge of their world, teetering back and forth like a tightrope walker in the circus. Beyond him was an awful black void that roared and screamed as it smashed into the liquid light—a void as dark and terrifying as the one Denise had experienced on her very first trip to Fayrah.

"Gus!" Denise warned, "get away from there!"

But Gus barely heard. The roar was too loud. Instead, he gave a grin, leaped high into the air, and made a perfect 360—well almost. Unfortunately his landing wasn't so perfect. His right foot slipped and he started to loose his balance.

"Noooo!" Denise screamed as she started for him.

But at the last second, Gus caught himself and turned to her laughing. "Listen, I don't know who you are, but you're gonna have to loosen up a little. Besides fallin' over the edge is the best part. Come on over here and give it a try."

Denise shook her head and shouted over the roar. "Gus, you've got to listen to me! You're going to—"

But Gus wasn't listening. If she wasn't interested in his little hobby, he'd find somebody who was. "Hey Gertie!" he called. "You oughta try this!"

Gertie just stood, panting and slowly sinking under her heavy burden. "No thanks . . ." she groaned, "I've got these signs to carry."

"Signs? What for?"

"They're from Denny—to make us happy. She wants us to carry them."

"No, that's not true!" Denise shouted.

"Happy?" Gus scoffed.

"Well, yeah!" Gertie shouted back a little defensively. "Carrying them makes you happy!"

"Right," he laughed. "Looks like you're havin' a terrific time!"

"They're not so bad, once you get used to them. Want to try one?"

"Forget it!" he called back. "If you're lookin' for good times, this here's the ticket!"

Gertie gave a doubtful look past him and into the roaring void.

"Don't worry about that!" he shouted. "It ain't as scary as it looks."

"I don't know," Gertie answered. Somehow the void didn't look too inviting.

"What's the matter?" he teased. "Chicken?"

"Maybe."

"Come on," he laughed, doing a quick little 180 hop. "You won't know till you try."

"Don't listen to him!" Denise shouted. "He doesn't know what he's doing!" There was no hiding the desperation in her voice. If Gertie joined Gus on the edge she would lose both of them. "I'm not there anymore!" she shouted. "I can't catch him! I can't catch you!"

"Come on, Gertie!" he called, giving a little hop and a spin on one foot. "Give it a shot, it's a real hoot!"

Although she tried to ignore him, Gertie found herself gradually beginning to listen.

"And you can bring them signs with you," he continued. "I mean, if you really think you have to."

"I can?"

"Gertie, no! Gus, please!"

"Sure," Gus answered as he leaped into the air, landing on all four hands. He did a little jig before hopping back to his feet. "C'mon, you won't know till you try it."

Gertie readjusted the load on her back. "You're really sure it's safe?"

"Hey, I'm still here, ain't I?"

"Gertie, no!"

Gertie threw Denise a quick glance then looked back to Gus. It had been a long time since she and Gus had played together but the memories were still fresh. Good memories, warm memories. Gus had never been anything but fun and he'd never done anything to hurt her. Why would he start now? Besides, she'd worked plenty hard serving Denny, and she felt entitled to a little relaxation. Finally she shouted, "All right!" and staggered toward him.

"NO!" Denise screamed. She leaped the few feet separating them and tackled Gertie to the ground. The signs fell heavily to the sand as the two rolled back and forth, all four feet kicking, all eight arms flying.

"LET GO—GIVE ME BACK MY SIGNS!" Gertie screamed. "LET GO OF ME!"

"LISTEN TO ME, GERTIE, LISTEN TO ME!"

Around and around they rolled while Gus looked on and laughed. This was great. Almost as much fun as edge-jumping!

"GERTIE, PLEASE . . ."

"I WANT MY SIGNS!"

"GERTIE . . ."

At last Gertie managed to grab the closest sign. As she pulled it to herself, Denise tried to make her let go of it.

"GERTIE . . ."

"MY SIGN . . ."

"GERTIE, LET ME HAVE IT."

Rolling onto her back, Gertie tucked her legs into her chest and suddenly kicked out. Her feet landed squarely in Denise's stomach, throwing her backward with an OOAAAF!

"Gertie," she gasped, trying to catch her breath. "PLEASE!" But Gertie was already reaching for the other sign. Denise lunged for her again.

This time Gertie was prepared—she had a weapon. Raising the sign high over her shoulder, she leaned back like a batter waiting for the perfect pitch.

* Denise saw what was about to happen and tried to stop. But the momentum in the liquid light kept her moving forward until suddenly, *SWOOOSH*, Gertie took the swing. The steel sign cut through the liquid. Its sharp

---

*This section may be too intense for reading to younger chidren. Please see the preface in *The Portal*.

corner caught Denise hard, ripping through her clothing and slicing deep into her side.

For a moment, Denny didn't know what had happened. She only saw the look of shock on Gertie's face. Then she felt something warm coming from her body. She looked down and noticed blood clouding the liquid all around her. Then she saw the gash in her side.

Finally there was the pain. It was sharp, searing, relentless. She slowly raised her eyes from the gaping hole to Gertie. Her friend's face was filled with horror.

No one spoke a word. Everything was silent as the liquid light grew more and more cloudy.

Denise tried to breathe, but every breath sent the sharp, jagged pain deeper into her body. Slowly the edges around her vision started to blur, growing white and fuzzy. Suddenly her legs were rubbery, but only for a second. They gave out all together and she crumpled to the ground.

"Ha!" Gus laughed. "Serves her right!"

Gertie continued to stare, horrified at what she had done—unsure of what she should do.

All this as the liquid light around them grew darker and darker . . .

CHAPTER TWELVE

REUNION

"Aristophenix! Listro Q!"

The group spun around to see Josh's little brother, Nathan. He had just popped in with his stuffed English bulldog, Mr. Hornsberry. They had one other companion: Samson, the half-dragonfly, half-ladybug who had become such good friends with Denny on their last journey together.

"Nathan!" Josh cried in surprise. "What are you doing here?"

"Samson says Denny's in some sort of trouble."

"But how'd you get here?"

Nathan held up another Cross-Dimensionalizer exactly like Listro Q's. "It's Samson's. He let me try it out. How'd I do?"

"Nice, very," Listro Q answered almost grudgingly. Then half under his breath he added, "Maybe lessons give me he should." Everyone chuckled, until Samson interrupted with a high squeal chatter.

Aristophenix answered:

Denny's in there,
dying for love.
But we're all out here,
'cause the door we can't shove.

Again Samson chattered.

This time Bud answered, "The fault is mine mine. I left the key key inside."

For a moment the group was unsure what to do. That is, until Mr. Hornsberry cleared his throat and spoke up. "I say, although no one is seeking my advice, would it not be advantageous for us to utilize all of our man and, er, dog power?"

"So how?" Listro Q asked.

"My good man," Mr. Hornsberry answered in his usual why-am-I-surrounded-by-morons tone of voice, "All we need to do is lift this door off its hinges."

As much as everyone hated to admit it, Mr. Hornsberry had a point. Now there was just the detail of how to do it. Unfortunately, every one had their own opinion and no one was afraid to voice it. The air was suddenly full of a hundred "if you ask me's," "no, we should try's," and "I'm tellin' you my way's better's."

On and on they argued as if each were some sort of master door remover. Of course none of them were, so nothing much happened—except more arguing. Then finally, ever so slowly, the door began to slide open by itself.

"What on earth . . . How do you suppose?"

At last they saw the reason: While everyone pretended to be an expert, Samson simply flew through the keyhole, unlatched the door from the inside, and with considerable effort pushed it open.

"All right, Sammy!" everyone shouted as they poured into the laboratory. But their celebration was short-lived. Denise was nowhere to be found.

"Bud, what's going on?" Josh demanded. "You said—"

"I know know," Bud answered as he picked up his pace and started running toward the Platform.

The group quickly followed, but when they arrived there was still no sign of her.

"Bud?" Josh repeated more urgently.

But Bud wasn't listening. "Machine!" he ordered.

The Machine hummed to life.

"Where is Denny?"

After a faint crackle a giant monitor slowly lowered from the ceiling. After another moment Denise's image flickered on the screen.

Everyone gasped, but not so much because of her four arms or because she was lying unconscious in the liquid light. They gasped at the bleeding wound in her side.

"DENNY!" Josh called. "DENNY!"

"She can't hear you you," Bud assured him.

"Look!" Josh shouted, releasing his full anger at Bud. "You got her into this mess, now you get her out!"

"I can't can't!" Bud stammered. "This was her decision, this was her—"

Suddenly Josh grabbed the little man by his shoulders and pulled him directly into his face. "I don't care whose decision it was!" he shouted. "Do what you have to do to save her!"

"But . . . but—"

"NOW!"

"The only way to save her is to to reduce someone to

her size size, so that they can rescue her."

"DO IT!" Josh shouted.

"But you don't understand how dangerous—"

"DO IT TO ME, NOW!" The fire in Josh's eyes told Bud he had no choice.

"Machine Machine," he called.

The Machine crackled in response.

"Take Joshua here and—"

> "UNTIL ALL IS ACCOMPLISHED,
> DO NOT INTERFERE."

The voice caught everyone off-guard. But it wasn't a voice exactly. It was more like a thought—a thought that vibrated inside everyone's head at the same time. Then it was gone.

Josh spun around to the rest of the group. Their mouths hung open in equal astonishment. "What—Who was that?" he said, lowering his voice.

For a moment no one answered. Then, after a nervous swallow, Bud finally spoke: "Imager."

Nobody said a word, not even Mr. Hornsberry. It was the strongest, most commanding voice they had ever heard and yet, at the same time, it was the gentlest and most soothing.

Then they heard another voice. "Please . . ." It was Denise. All eyes shot up to the monitor and watched. She had regained consciousness and was dragging her bleeding body toward two other multi-armed creatures. "Gus," she gasped, "Gertie."

But the creatures did not answer. Instead the bigger one ordered the smaller to hit Denise. At first the smaller hesitated. But as Denny continued to approach them, the bigger one kept urging until the smaller one raised the steel signs high overhead and brought them down hard on Denise's back.

Everyone in the laboratory cried out at the blow.

But Denise wouldn't stop. She slowly rose to her hands and knees and started toward them again. "Please . . ."

Once again she was clobbered with the signs.

That was it. Josh could take no more. That was his friend up there on the screen and he wasn't going to sit around and watch her being beaten to death. Imager or not, he began to shout at the thought or the voice or whatever it was: "What type of logic is this!"

There was no response, only silence—and nervous coughs among the group.

"Answer me!"

Silence.

"You claim to be so logical, so loving—so answer me! ANSWER ME!"

Finally the voice in their heads spoke. But it wasn't angry. It was tender and understanding. It was also firm—very firm.

"UNTIL ALL IS ACCOMPLISHED,
DO NOT INTERFERE."

"BUT SHE'S DYING!" Josh shouted. "SHE'S KILL-ING HERSELF! WHERE'S THE LOGIC? ANSWER ME! ANSWER ME!"

The answer rang loud and clear, and very, very gentle:

"UNTIL ALL IS ACCOMPLISHED,
DO NOT INTERFERE."

"UNTIL WHAT IS ACCOMPLISHED? HOW WILL WE KNOW? WHAT CAN WE DO?"

There was no answer.

"HOW WILL WE KNOW?!" Josh repeated.

But the voice had said all that was necessary. Now there was only silence.

Josh let out a sigh of frustration and turned to the others. Everyone looked equally baffled and confused—everyone but Samson.

The little fellow flew closer to the Platform and waited. His heart had always been the closest to Denny's. He knew that from the moment they first met. Although they were two very different creatures from two very different dimensions, they were very much alike. And although no signal would be given, somehow Samson would know. When the time was right, he knew he would know.

Not another word was said. Imager had spoken—three times. There was nothing to do now but obey. Watch and obey. All eyes returned to the monitor and waited.

---

* As Gertie continued to clutch the signs, their weight continued to crush her body forcing her deeper and deeper into the sand. But that was nothing compared to the pain those signs had caused Denny. Not only was the gash in Denny's side still pouring blood into the liquid light, but thanks to Gus's insistence, Gertie had hit her with the signs again and again.

Still, nothing would stop Denise. No matter how many times Gertie hit her and no matter how great the pain, Denny still continued toward them. Granted, each time she rose, she rose a little slower, but she still continued to rise. She had to save Gus and Gertie—nothing else mattered.

By now they were backed up against the edge, just a

few feet from the roaring, black emptiness. "Please . . ." Denny whispered hoarsely. "Please . . ."

"What do you want?" Gertie screamed. "What do you want from us?"

"I want . . . I want you to live . . ."

"You're a loon!" Gus shouted. "We *are* living!"

Denise shook her head and with great effort reached for the signs. "Please . . ."

"Hit her again!" Gus shouted over the roaring void. "If she wants those signs so bad, let her have 'em again—only this time don't hold back. This time give her everything you got!"

Gertie didn't like the idea, not one bit. She was already crying over the pain she had caused. How could she inflict any more?

Still, something had to be done.

"Go ahead," Gus urged. "Everything you got!"

It went against all that Gertie believed, but she knew she had to do something to stop Denise.

"Go ahead. Don't hold back."

Otherwise, it would go on like this forever. Denny would never give them rest.

"Go ahead, Gertie. Go ahead."

Finally, Gertie lifted the signs overhead. She leaned back, closed her eyes, and . . .

"NO!"

Gus was the first to spot the Illusionist. She stood on top of the Wall. To him she was the most exciting thing he had ever seen. Not that she was beautiful, it was more than that. There was a wildness about her—a kind of courage. To Gus she appeared to be everything he admired, and more.

To Gertie she appeared to be just the opposite—sweet, understanding, sensitive. It was a neat trick, appearing as two different people at the same time, but the creature hadn't earned the name *Illusionist* for nothing.

"Who are you?" Gus called.

"She's our friend," Gertie answered. "The one who taught us about free will."

Denise heard them but didn't have the strength to turn around. She didn't have to, she knew who it was. "Don't listen to her," she croaked, reaching up and clinging to Gertie's sleeves. "She'll kill—"

"DESTROY HER!" the Illusionist shrieked.

"What?" Gus asked, a little surprised at the sudden outburst.

The Illusionist cleared her throat and quickly regained control. "It's only a suggestion. After all, I don't want to interfere with your free will. But if you ask me, hitting her is not enough. You must destroy her by rolling her off the edge."

"But she'll come back," Gus explained. "I always have."

The Illusionist gave him a sinister grin. "Trust me. She won't come back—not this time."

"Why?" Gertie asked, a little confused. "Why do we have to destroy her?"

"It's for her own good," the Illusionist suddenly cooed. While speaking to Gertie, it was important she use the sweetest, most understanding voice she could muster. "It's the kindest thing to do, dear child. Otherwise she'll keep coming at you and you'll have to keep hurting her."

Gertie looked down at Denise and was moved with pity. It was true. Gertie had inflicted more pain than she'd ever thought possible. But no matter how much Denise bled, no matter how many times Gertie hit her, Denny would not give up. It was pathetic. Maybe the

Illusionist was right. Maybe it was best to put her out
of her misery.

"Let's face it," the Illusionist sneered (this time for
Gus's sake), "the wretched thing has no pride. If you
don't destroy her, she'll always be pestering you. Just
look at the way her blood is darkening your perfect
ocean; look at the way she never gives you a moment's
rest."

It was Gus's turn to stare at Denise. The Illusionist
was right. Denise was ruining their ocean. And if they
didn't put her away for good, her constant nagging and
begging would drive them crazy.

"Go ahead," the Illusionist insisted. "Gertie, you can
keep those perfect signs forever. And Gus, you can jump
off the edge anytime you want. No one will stop either
of you."

"No one?" they asked in unison.

"Certainly not me," the Illusionist grinned. "I
wouldn't dream of stopping you!"

Again the two glanced at each other.

Denise no longer had the strength to cry out. She
could only shake her head, pleading to them with her
eyes.

The Illusionist did her best to stifle a yawn. "When
you stop to think about it, you really have no other
choice."

Gus was the first to agree. "Grab her arms," he ordered Gertie.

"There's no other way?" Gertie asked, her voice full
of sympathy.

"You heard her, didn't you?"

Gertie nodded and looked sadly at Denise. The Illusionist was right; she had to be put out of her misery.
After a moment's hesitation, Gertie slowly stooped

down. "I'm sorry," she whispered, but it really is for your best." Still holding her signs high above with one set of arms, Gertie took Denise's head into her other hands. Gently she stroked it. "Maybe . . . Maybe if you'd stop trying to help us . . . Maybe, if you'd just let us have our way instead of always . . ."

But Denise shook her head. She opened her mouth to explain, but all she could manage was a wheezing gasp.

Slowly, sadly, Gertie rose to her feet. "I'm sorry," she repeated, "I'm so sorry." Then, taking Denise's arms with her two free hands she gently raised her off the ground.

Denise clenched her eyes shut, the pain was too great. But it was not the pain of her wounds, or even the thought of being destroyed. It was the pain of a broken heart.

She felt Gus pick up her feet. Now, she was suspended between them.

"On the count of three," Gus ordered.

Three times they swung her out over the edge . . . and back.

"One . . ."

"Two . . ."

But on the third count, using what little strength she had, Denise lunged toward the signs in Gertie's other two hands. It was a desperate attempt. Still, she managed to catch the edges of the two steel plates and hung on for dear life. Nothing would make her let go.

But the extra weight of the signs gave the final swing an extra momentum that Gus and Gertie could not control. Denise slipped out of their hands and fell helplessly into the roaring void.

Denise had lost. There was no mistaking it. She was heading for her death. But even as she tumbled and fell into a blackness that grew darker and colder, even as the roar of destruction shrieked in her ears, Denise couldn't help but feel at peace. She may have lost, but she also had the signs. Pulling them closer to her chest, she couldn't stop the smile from spreading across her face. For even though it had cost Denny her life, her love had prevailed. She had lost, yes. But she had also won.

— CHAPTER THIRTEEN —

TO THE RESCUE

The group screamed as Denise fell.

Everyone but Samson.

While the others had been staring at the monitor high overhead, Samson hovered near the Platform, carefully searching the liquid light. He had spotted the slight ripples near the edge from Gus and Gertie's movements. As soon as Denny fell from their hands, Samson made his move.

"Samson! What are you doing?" Nathan shouted. "Samson!"

But it was too late. He had no time to explain. Imager had said, "Until all is accomplished . . ." Well, as far as he could tell *all* had been accomplished. Now the little guy couldn't waste a second.

He swooped toward the Platform's edge. And just as Denise had done so many times with Gus, Samson managed to spot the tiny pinpoint glimmer of her reflection and raced toward it.

Faster and faster she fell.

Swifter and swifter he flew.

Finally he was in position. Quickly he swooped under her. But they were traveling too fast. Although she landed briefly on his back, Denny's inertia forced her to tumble and roll until she shot off the other side . . . and continued to fall.

Samson spun around and dove after her.

The floor was coming up fast.

Common sense told Samson to pull out of the dive before it was too late. If he didn't, they'd both be smashed to bits. *It's better to lose one life than two.* That's what his mind was saying. But Samson's heart was bigger than his mind.

He folded back his wings and dove even faster.

The floor was closer now . . . much, much closer.

At last he was even with Denise. In another second he would be able to get past her, swoop underneath, and let her land on his back again. Unfortunately, they didn't have another second.

As a last act of desperation, Samson unfolded his right wing and thrust it into the roaring wind toward Denny. The rushing air screamed and tugged at the wing, nearly ripping it out of its socket, but Samson endured the pain. He continued to stretch out the wing until it was finally beneath her.

Then he felt it—Denny's tiny presence hitting his wing. In a flash, and with only one wing to maneuver, Samson reversed course and zoomed upward. It was close. In fact, he had actually felt the lab's cold floor brush against his hind legs as he pulled up. But he made it!

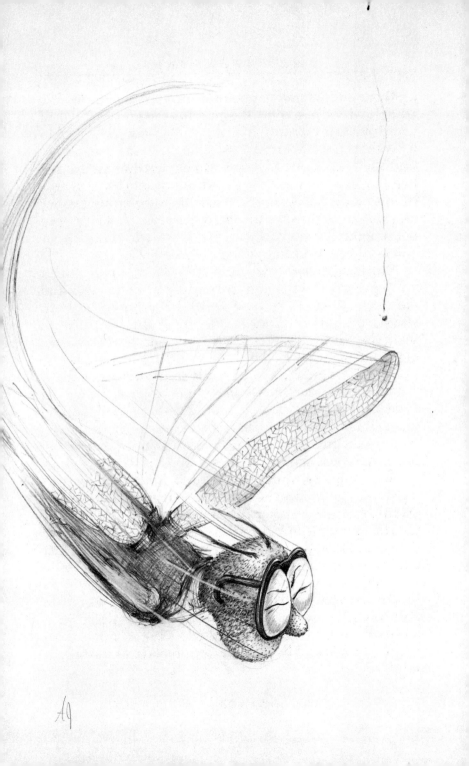

Denise and the signs had crashed hard onto Samson's wing, and for a second the breath was knocked out of her. But Denny didn't complain. She was glad just to have breath to be knocked out. Of course, she was so tiny that she had no idea what had happened or where she had landed. As far as she could tell, it felt like she was riding some kind of giant elevator the way it quickly shot upward. Yet it was the strangest elevator she'd ever been on. It seemed to have a gauzy, almost transparent floor and a huge, flickering red light at the back.

But Denise had little time to wonder, for in just a matter of seconds the Platform came back into view. And there, standing on its edge were Gus and Gertie—both staring out at her in amazement. On the Wall behind them the Illusionist was jumping up and down screaming what she screamed best: "Unfair, unfair, unfair!"

For a moment, Samson slowed and gently approached the edge for Denise to get a better look. Gus and Gertie were so close she could have reached out and touched them, if she'd had the strength.

"Unfair, unfair!" the Illusionist continued to scream. But no one was paying any attention to her.

"I'll be back," Denise tried to call out, but she was too weak. Her voice was only a whisper—barely audible over the roar of the void. Still, somehow the two seemed to understand. Gertie was the first to nod. Then slowly, almost reluctantly, Gus joined in. And then—was it just her imagination, or had the slightest trace of a smile crossed both their faces? Denise wasn't sure.

Gently, very gently, Samson began to rise away from the Platform. Gus and Gertie slowly shrank in size until they were nothing but tiny little dots.

"I'll be back," Denny repeated, mostly to herself. "I promise, I'll be—" But that was all she remembered. The emotions were too intense, the pain too overwhelming. She collapsed into a deep and much needed sleep.

———

For the next several days Denise did little but eat and sleep. Once the Machine had changed her back to normal size, the group had whisked her out of the lab and off to Samson's home in Fayrah. Here she would rest until she was strong enough to head back home. "Your mind and your body have been through a terrible trauma," the doctor had explained, "and now both need time to rest and heal."

"But, what about Mom, what about Josh's grandpa?" Denise had protested. "They'll be worried sick."

"Worry, not to," Listro Q assured her from across the room.

"The ol' boy's right," Aristophenix added. "Remember . . .

We're running in time
much faster than you reckon.
And for us, what's a week,
to them's but a second.

"Right is he," Listro Q agreed. "Teapot remember the, in Grandpa's shop that you dropped?"

"The one that floated?"

Listro Q nodded. "Floating, still is it."

Denise looked at him in amazement. But before she could say anything, Violet, Samson's new bride, had buzzed in and began chattering a mile a second.

"What's she saying?" Denise asked.

Aristophenix gave a hasty explanation:

She's saying it's her house,
and there isn't a doubt

you'll be getting some rest,
'cause she's kicking us out!

Denise couldn't hold back a giggle as she watched
Violet buzz and dive-bomb the guests sitting around the
bedroom.

"All right, we're going, we're going!" they shouted,
raising their arms and stumbling toward the door.
"Come on, lady, give us a break. Samson, will you call
her off!"

But Samson didn't call her off and Violet didn't stop
until every one of them was out of the bedroom.

"That's quite a wife you have," Denise said, grinning
at Samson.

Samson chattered back a proud reply, but was cut
short as he, too, was shooed out of the room.

That had been nearly a week ago. Six days had passed
before the doctor finally gave Denise permission to
travel. And once word spread that they were going, Samson's front room and yard were filled with hundreds of
well-wishers and *bon-voyagers*. Some of them had never
even met Denise, but they'd all heard of her deeds.

"Now you take care of this side," the doctor warned
as he changed the dressing and bandages on her wound
for the last time. "It will be awhile before it is completely
healed."

Denise nodded.

"And I'm afraid you'll always have a scar," the doctor
added, "quite a large one."

Denise looked down at the red, jagged line that ran
from the middle of her ribs all the way to her hip. "That's
OK," she said quietly, "it'll help me remember." Then,
before she knew it, tears began to fall—just as they had
so many times throughout the week.

"Thinking about Gus and Gertie again?" Josh gently

asked as he sat down beside her on the bed.

She gave a quick nod and tried to brush the tears away. "And Imager too," she mumbled. Looking up, she spotted Aristophenix and Listro Q standing nearby. She continued softly, "He really does care for us, doesn't he?"

They nodded in silence.

"I mean if he only feels a *part* of what I felt for Gus and Gertie . . ." her voice trailed off in thought.

"More," Listro Q gently added, "more many times, for us each."

Denise could only shake her head in amazement. "How can he bear it?" she whispered to herself. "The joy . . . the pain . . ." Once again the group fell silent as Denise unconsciously touched the wound in her side . . . "How can he stand it?"

"Step back, please . . . coming through, yes we are." The silence was shattered by the brash entrance of the Weaver. Following behind were two of his assistants, each of them carrying an easel and small tapestry. And behind them poured all the folks who had been patiently waiting in the front room, the yard, and throughout much of Fayrah. The Weaver's presence always brought crowds of curious onlookers. Before they knew it, Denise's room was so packed that no amount of buzzing and dive-bombing by Violet could unpack it.

"Oh, there you are," the Weaver shouted to Denise above the noise. "Getting better are we? Good!" Turning back to his assistants he called, "Just set those up anywhere, boys."

"What . . . what are you doing here?' Denise asked.

"Rumor has it you're pretty concerned about Gus and Gertie, yes you are. Well, no need to be. I brought their tapestries along to show you before you go."

"Gus and Gertie had tapestries?" Denise asked in astonishment.

"Of course! You don't think I'd let something that important slip by, do you?"

"Well no, I guess—"

"So tell me," he interrupted, proudly pointing to the tapestries, each on their own easel, "what do you think?"

They were more beautiful than Denise could have imagined. Each thread shimmered and danced in the light. Each design perfectly captured their personalities. In fact, the patterns were so perfect that as she stared at them Denise could almost see and hear Gus and Gertie again. Unfortunately, this only brought on another grimace of pain and more tears.

"Ah, come on, they're not that ugly," the Weaver protested.

Denise shook her head. "Oh, no . . . they were beautiful . . . wonderful . . ."

"What do you mean *were*? You can see for yourself both Gus and Gertie will be living for many more epochs, and—"

"They're still alive?" Denise cried. The others in the room also started to buzz.

"Well, yes of course," the Weaver continued, "as are their children and their children's children and their—"

"They have children, too?"

Once again the Weaver tried to overlook the interruption. "Of course, thousands of them. And according to this thread here—"

"They have thousands of children?"

"If you keep interrupting me, child" the Weaver said evenly, "we won't get through this before you leave."

Denise nodded. Her mind reeled with excitement. She'd just naturally thought that Gus would have talked Gertie into jumping off the edge with him. But the fact that they were still alive, and that they actually had children, well, the possibility made her so excited that she could barely listen.

"Now, where was I?" the Weaver asked. "Oh, yes. This thread, here," he said, pointing to the first tapestry, "indicates Gus's continual fascination with the edge. But, instead of leaping off, he has taken Gertie's advice and has devoted his life to studying it."

"Studying it?" Denise asked.

"Yes, scientific evaluation, I believe they call it."

"Gus has become a *scientist*?"

"Yes, well, I'm afraid Bud has taken over leadership while you're away, and he has had some impact upon—"

"Oh, no," Josh groaned good-naturedly, "Bud is their leader?"

"I hope he doesn't drop anything on them," Denise giggled.

Everyone else in the room also chuckled. Apparently Bud's reputation for grace had spread far and wide.

The Weaver went on, "And just as Gus has continued his scientific studies, Gertie has been writing and teaching her children poetry."

Denise kept on listening, trying to grasp the words. The news was so good. So very, very good.

"And do you see this deep scarlet thread here?" the Weaver asked the group as he pointed to a deep red thread. "This is most intriguing. See how it runs through the center of both patterns, seeming to hold them together?"

Everyone in the room nodded.

He turned directly to Denise. "That red thread is you, my girl, yes it is. You are what they speak of in science class. You are what they write about in their poetry."

Suddenly Denise broke into laughter—and tears.

"Good gracious, *now* what is it?" the Weaver demanded.

"I'm sorry," Denise said, grinning sheepishly while trying to wipe her eyes. "It's just . . . well, the thing is. . . ." she tried to explain but couldn't. Everything was just too good, too perfect. And, well, that meant laughter . . . and it meant tears.

But it wasn't only Denise. It seemed everyone in the room had suddenly come down with a good case of smiles and sniffles—everyone but Mr. Hornsberry. After all, stuffed dogs know better than to cry—they mildew.

"I say there," the stodgy animal said, clearing his throat in his usual snooty manner, "what about that dreadful Illusionist creature? Where is she in their tapestries?"

"Right here," the Weaver said pointing to a dark thread. "As you can see, she makes an appearance from time to time, but her effect upon the overall work is minimal at best, yes it is."

"But Denny's thread," Josh interrupted, "it keeps showing up in both of them, all the way to the end."

"Correct. They will remember her life throughout their civilization . . . passing her exploits down from one generation to the next. In fact, to this day, they claim she is the one responsible for the remarkable rose hue that subtly colors their ocean. They say this is to remind them of her love as well as her promise to return one day. A promise," he turned to Denise, "that as their creator you are bound to keep."

Denise nodded eagerly. There would be no problem keeping that promise. In fact, she wouldn't mind keeping it right now. But she knew that was out of the question. For now, at least, she would have to return home with the others.

"That's all I've got to say," the Weaver concluded. "You'd better get a move on, yes you'd better. If I remember your patterns correctly, you'll be leaving here in," he glanced at his wristwatch, "less than 48 seconds."

The room exploded into action. Everyone ran around hugging, shouting thank you's, saying goodbyes, and making the usual promises to stay in touch.

It was during this confusion that Josh pulled the Weaver aside. "Listen," he said, "I just want to thank you. I know I was a bit of a pain, not believing and everything."

"Most of you are," the Weaver chuckled, "but we're getting used to it."

Josh gave a half-smile and continued, "If you could tell Bud thanks for me, too—I didn't get to say much when we rushed Denny out of there and everything. But he really did help me . . . a lot."

"You'll get a chance to thank him yourself," the Weaver answered. "Yes, you will."

"What? " Josh was a little astonished. "When?"

The Weaver lowered his voice slightly and glanced around the room to make sure he wasn't being overheard. "I shouldn't say anything, but he will be cross-dimensionalizing over to your world soon . . . very soon."

"Well . . . well that's great!"

The Weaver scowled slightly. "Perhaps, but with him will come the Illusionist, and also your little brother's enemy, Bobok."

"To our kingdom—to Earth?"

The Weaver nodded.

"But . . . I mean . . . we'll still be OK and everything, right?"

The Weaver took a deep breath. For a moment it looked like he would answer, then suddenly he changed his mind. "I've said too much already."

"Oh, come on!" Josh pleaded.

"Josh, go let's!" It was Listro Q shouting. He had grouped all those heading back to the Upside-down Kingdom at the other end of the room.

But Josh paid little attention. He was still searching the Weaver's face. "You've got to tell me *something*."

"Just . . . be careful. It is a most clever plan."

"But, we'll be all right?" Josh again insisted.

"Go let's, come on Josh . . ." By now the others had started to pull him away, leading him to the group. With a few more tugs and jostles, they finally got him into place alongside Denise, Nathan, Mr. Hornsberry, Aristophenix, and Listro Q. Josh immediately scanned the crowd for the Weaver. But the man was nowhere to be found. Somehow, Josh was not surprised.

"All righty!" Aristophenix shouted.

Let's move, let's go,
let's have no more stops.
It's straight from Fayrah,
to Grandpa's Secondhand Shop.

"Goodbye," everyone began to shout. "See you later . . . bye-bye . . ."

Denise caught Samson's and Violet's eyes. It was too noisy to be heard, so she mouthed the words, "Thank you."

Both insects understood and flickered their red taillights in response.

Listro Q reached for his Cross-Dimensionalizer and prepared to punch in the coordinates.

"Need any help with that?" Nathan teased.

"Manage think I can," Listro Q grinned back as he pushed the four buttons.

BEEP . . .
    BOP . . .
        BURP . . .
            BLEEP . . .

Unfortunately, the sounds were immediately followed by others:
CRASH, BANG, BOOM, CLATTER, CLATTER, TINKLE.

Everyone in the room cringed. Although no one in Fayrah could see it, there was no ignoring the fact that Listro Q had once again missed his landing coordinates. Granted, it was only by a few feet, but a few feet in Grandpa O'Brien's cluttered Secondhand Shop was as good as a mile. By the sound of things, they must have wound up in the pots and pans display in the window.

But that's OK. Over the months and years, Listro Q would have plenty more opportunities to get his coordinates right for traveling to that shop.

Plenty more. . . .